BEST
LESBIAN ROMANCE
OF THE YEAR

VOLUME ONE

BEST
LESBIAN ROMANCE
OF THE YEAR

VOLUME ONE

Edited by

RADCLYFFE

CLEiS
PRESS

Published in the United States by Cleis Press, an imprint of Start Midnight, LLC, 375 Hudson Street, Twelfth Floor, New York, New York, 10014.

Printed in the United States.
Cover design: Scott Idleman/Blink
Cover photograph: iStockphoto
Text design: Frank Wiedemann

First Edition.

Trade paper ISBN: 978-1-62778-087-2
E-book ISBN: 978-1-62778-102-2

CONTENTS

vii Introduction

1 Some Nudity Required • AXA LEE
18 Light • DESTINY MOON
26 Red Velvet Cake • TAMSIN FLOWERS
36 Unexpected Bliss • GUN BROOKE
46 Waterfall • LT MASTERS
63 Love Dance • MERINA CANYON
76 Like a Breath of Ocean Blue • ELIZABETH BLACK
90 Wiggle-Wiggle-Womp • D. JACKSON LEIGH
100 Long Drive • L.C. SPOERING
109 Dance Fever • KARA A. MCLEOD
124 Cooling Down, Heating Up • DENA HANKINS
136 Little Bit of Ivory • JL MERROW
141 A Royal Engagement • NELL STARK
150 Gargoyle Lovers • SACCHI GREEN
155 Going to the Chapel • GISELLE RENARDE
170 Forever Yours, Eileen • REBEKAH WEATHERSPOON
185 Beautiful • TERESA NOELLE ROBERTS
189 Bad Girls and Sweet Kisses • RADCLYFFE

199 About the Authors
203 About the Editor

INTRODUCTION

Audre Lorde has said, "There are no new ideas. There are only new ways of making them felt."[1] Romance fiction, like every literary form, has identifiable elements that are intrinsic to the genre and without which a work would not be considered a romance. The simplest definition of a romance is that put forth by the Romance Writers of America, an organization that has defined the romance as "a work of fiction containing a central love story that results in an emotionally satisfying and optimistic ending."[2] While this broad categorization helps distinguish between works focused on a developing love relationship (i.e., romances) and ones that do not, the elements of the genre itself are not defined. Pamela Regis's *A Natural History of the Romance Novel* studies a number of classic romances and finds that certain themes are identifiable in each one. This was the first work to critically analyze and enumerate the essential elements of a romance, which as defined by Regis, include Society Defined, The Meeting, The Barrier, The Attraction, The

Declaration, Point of Ritual Death, The Recognition and The Betrothal.[3] What is important to understand in considering these elements is that the romance *reader* recognizes the elements of the romantic journey unconsciously, searches for these elements and is not satisfied if they are absent. The short form is by necessity a distillation of the romantic journey present in a romance novel, and what I find fascinating is that short stories with a romance theme often represent one or more of these essential elements, presenting to the reader a recognizable, satisfying aspect of the romantic journey.

Some stories focus on the initial meeting, those first moments of enchantment, excitement, and connection that occur when we meet, by chance or design, and discover, as in Axa Lee's "Some Nudity Required," someone totally unexpected:

> Audra glanced up from her note taking, giving me an inscrutable look. She was beautiful, but not in a classic way. Much of it, I thought, came from the energy she vibrated. Her nose was too long and slightly hooked, and her teeth weren't completely white or straight. Her appeal lay in her vivaciousness, that inexplicable *something* that some people have and I didn't. There was a certain spark in her, an intelligence in her eyes, laugh lines around her mouth, that said "look at me."
>
> She didn't try not to be noticed.

Often following close upon the meeting is the awareness of attraction—it may develop slowly or be instantaneous, but stories focused on the developing and irresistible attraction, as in Destiny Moon's "Light," are another step in the journey to romantic fulfillment.

Two hours later, I felt like I'd known her my whole life. It's incredible how whole she felt to me, how deep and multifaceted. There was so much more to her than what was visible on the surface...I'd seen her around. I'd noticed the way she held the door open for Tania, how she doted on her, how sweet she seemed. But I didn't really notice, didn't really see.

Until now. Now all I could do was see. She was right here in front of me...

The journey itself is not necessarily linear or the same for every work of fiction, just as it is not the same for individuals in real life. Not every couple faces challenging obstacles to being together, but when we read love stories, we are seeking the affirmation that love gives us strength and hope and courage, and the ability to overcome old fears, heal old wounds and sometimes enlighten prejudices and change the hearts and minds of those who might seek to keep us apart. Conflict resolution is another element of the romance genre that we see played out in stories like Kara A. McLeod's "Dance Fever," in which two women with a past take the first steps toward a new future:

She wanted us to leave. Together.

I gaped at her. Her blatant desire confused me. Even when we'd been a couple, she'd never wanted anyone to see us leaving a party together. We'd always had to leave separately with at least thirty minutes between our departure times, regardless of the fact that we were going to end up spending the night in each other's arms. I hesitated, not wanting to make the wrong assumption.

Allison smiled at me again, probably reading my

uncertainty loud and clear, and extended a hand to me. Tentatively, I reached out and took it. One night wouldn't be enough, but it might be a new beginning.

Of course, not every love story ends happily, but the power of romantic fiction lies in the creation of emotional bonds between characters that are strong enough and authentic enough to convince the reader that *for these characters in these circumstances,* love will prevail and continue. The declaration and commitment we look for in our romances remind us that the human heart is capable of tremendous resilience and courage, and that love can truly last a lifetime. Several of the eighteen short stories in this collection celebrate this commitment with a wedding—the public affirmation of trust and promise that, indeed, seals the love story with a kiss. All the elements critical to the romantic journey can be found in these short stories, each new, each unique and each recognizable, calling on emotions common to every human heart. I hope you enjoy these stories as they take you on another romantic journey.

Radclyffe
2015

Endnotes

1   Audre Lorde. BrainyQuote.com, Xplore Inc., 2014. brainyquote.com/ quotes/quotes/a/audrelorde124563.html, accessed June 2, 2014.
2   rwa.org/p/cm/ld/fid=578, accessed June 2, 2014.
3   Pamela Regis. *A Natural History of the Romance Novel.* University of Pennsylvania Press (2011).

SOME NUDITY REQUIRED

Axa Lee

She said she wanted to watch me—that was it.

If I'd had a landline, I'd have been wrapping and unwrapping the phone cord around my hand. Instead I paced through the apartment, picking things up and attempting to tidy the clutter before setting them back where they'd been, pressing my cell phone hard against my ear. I dislike talking on the phone, but the ad said no texts, and I didn't want to miss or misunderstand anything.

"Would Tuesday at two work for you?"

"Tuesday? Um, sure. I have a class, but it's in the morning." Unlike most college students, I loved 8 A.M. English.

My geek girl is showing, I know.

"All right, great." That distracted, overly enthusiastic tone of voice made it sound like she was writing something down. Or maybe she really was that enthusiastic. I guess no one would strip and pose for nude photographs with an angry, brooding person. "Well, I'll see you then." Her professional smile practically glowed through the phone.

We hung up and panic set in.

I'm not an exhibitionist. I'm not even an extrovert. I'm a nerdy, quiet, librarian type who gets feedback from professors that says, "Participate more in class discussion; EXCELLENT ESSAYS!!" So responding to an ad in the college paper for "Female Model, any body type, thesis project, some nudity required. Paying. Contact Audra," was not just out of character for me, but almost out of ken.

"You'll never do that," Erika said.

I tugged the newspaper back across the table, glaring at it rather than at her.

"How do you know?" I sounded sullen.

In the background, the cappuccino and coffee machines spat and steamed.

Erika liked to meet in public, saying it didn't look suspicious since most academics have a caffeine addiction. I told myself that at least if she wouldn't acknowledge me, she wasn't hiding me. After all, the best student in class had a right to meet with her TA outside of hours, right? It didn't mean that everyone knew we were sleeping together.

She didn't look up from the papers she was grading.

"I see students come through here year after year. Girls like you, they become museum curators or librarians, not models."

Erika looked like an English professor—thick black-rimmed glasses, wash-and-wear haircut, fitted button-down shirt, funky but not too funky jewelry. If she was a man, she'd have worn tweed and had a little mustache and goatee. Erika was very good at being what people expected. The problem was she expected the same behavior from her partner. And while I was by no means a rebel, that didn't mean I always wanted to conform.

"I'm already a librarian," I said, but she didn't hear me. Erika loved to hear herself talk. That was why she made a great academic. She'd been unofficially advising me on where to apply to grad school, but lately I'd been floundering. Something didn't feel right and I couldn't put my finger on what. But when I saw the ad for a model, I couldn't explain it; I just suddenly wanted very much to call Audra (what a great name!). I wanted to prove to myself that I could do something risky and out-of-character, like model nude, before college was over.

The question was, could I?

I showed up at Audra's apartment a little before two. I'm the type who's pathologically early. I lingered outside for all of forty-five seconds before becoming convinced everyone on the street was staring and suspicious (no one noticed me, they never do) and went up to knock. The woman who answered was shorter than me, maybe five or ten years older, and had white, spiky hair. She was fit and totally rocked a blocky pair of black and pink nerd girl glasses.

"I'm working on a graduate exhibition for my MFA," Audra said, after ushering me inside and moving swiftly through the necessary small talk. "I want to work with a model, chronicle something about her." She studied me, as a painter studies a canvas. "Can you tell me more about yourself?"

She gestured to one of the kitchen bar stools and filled each of us a glass of water. Normally I'd be too shy to accept beverages at someone's house, but my mouth had grown very dry.

And as my mouth grew dry, my pussy grew wet.

I crossed my legs, feeling the moisture soak my panties. Normally I'm very controlled. I try to be appropriate. But Audra's verve just got me, very suddenly and very inexplicably.

How would I get through a nude photo shoot with her when I couldn't even tell her my major without creaming? Shakespeare's shoes, what was I getting into?

"Um, not much to tell really." I spoke carefully, more carefully than usual. Outgoing, dynamic people intimidate me, precisely because I'm not one. "I'm an English major, senior, honors, so I'll be working on my senior project, probably something to do with twentieth-century poets." I glossed over that. "And applying to grad schools. I work at the library."

"Do you have a partner?" Audra glanced up from her note taking, giving me an inscrutable look. She was beautiful, but not in a classic way. Much of it, I thought, came from the energy she vibrated. Her nose was too long and slightly hooked, and her teeth weren't completely white or straight. Her appeal lay in her vivaciousness, that inexplicable *something* that some people have and I didn't. There was a certain spark in her, an intelligence in her eyes, laugh lines around her mouth, that said "look at me."

She didn't try not to be noticed.

I'd almost forgotten the question.

"Yes," I said, nodding. Inside, I winced. I hated admitting Erika into the realm of this vibrant, attractive woman. "Sort of. She's a bit of an asshole."

Audra chuckled and patted my arm. "Aren't we all, luv?"

She was smiling at me. Her touch lingered, longer, perhaps, than socially necessary. I didn't like for people to touch me, but found I didn't mind that she did. And when Audra drew away and was up moving again—she seemed perpetually in motion—where her hand had lingered on my arm still tingled.

Audra was in the next room, a living room of sorts that was open to the kitchen. I followed her there as she tugged furniture and oversized white blocks here and there and then stood back to examine the positioning before tweaking something this way or that.

"Do you have a particular poet in mind for your thesis?" She frowned, changed her mind and started pushing everything out of the way again.

"Elizabeth Bishop?"

She glanced at me over her shoulder, smirking a little. "Are you asking or telling me?"

I smiled. "Both, maybe."

Audra stood back, hands on hips, Wonder Woman pose, eyeing her handiwork.

"That line about crumbs and coffee..." She snapped her fingers, trying to jog her memory. "I can't remember all of it, something about a window and misplaced miracle?"

I quoted the line.

"That's it!" she said. "I love that line. You must know a *ton* of Bishop poems. Which are your favorites?"

It was impossible not to feel comfortable with this woman. She had a knack for chatter, a way of making you feel comfortable.

"I actually like a quote from her letters the best—the one she wrote to Robert Lowell. That image of a sandpiper, always running, always looking for something along coastlines had haunted me for years. She's so...I don't know, appropriate? I love that about her. No matter what melodramatic bullshit he throws at her, she keeps her wits about her."

"Sometimes isn't acting on love more important than being appropriate?"

I shook my head. "I don't think so. If they'd gotten together they'd have made each other miserable. It's much better that she kept her head and didn't get swept up in his..."

"Romanticism?"

"Shenanigans."

"That's a fusty word for a college girl."

I shrugged.

Audra smiled, but ceded the point to me. Then she grew more serious, observing me steadily. "I like you," she said.

A thrill shot straight through my clenching pelvis.

"I'd like to work with you. There's amazing potential in you as a subject..." She bit her lip as she tucked a strand of hair behind my ear. "You've never been photographed before?"

I barked a laugh and spoke, too loudly. "I've never done *anything* like this before."

"A sustained project like this isn't just about the photographer. It's a journey for the subject as well. You've seen my work." She gestured to the select photos of black-and-white nudes hanging on the walls. "So this will be incredibly intimate. My goal with a subject like you isn't just to create a portfolio of my own work, but to uncover something in you. Like an archeologist." She smiled. "Art is supposed to teach us something about ourselves, after all. I'd like to make sure you feel comfortable with what we're going to do, how the process works. Because if you don't feel comfortable, it's not going to be fun for you and we want that. And it'll show on camera. We *don't* want that." She clapped her hands together once, smiling fiendishly. "Now, strip."

I sat on a futon mattress Audra had dragged from her bedroom and remade on the living room floor. We'd tried several poses with the blocks and furniture, but neither of us had seemed particularly at ease, even after Audra encouraged me to slip out of my jeans and said she'd do her best to hide my face.

"Celebrities might get away with sex tapes, but that might be awkward for an English major when the grad program director Googles you at Berkeley."

"Who knows," I said, "if it makes me stand out maybe it'll get me tenured." Milton knew, my thesis wouldn't get the job done.

Audra chuckled as she continued setting up the camera. She had a great smile. The butterflies in my stomach calmed when she smiled.

"Just move how you feel comfortable," Audra had said.

I'd snorted. I *so* did not feel comfortable. Maybe Erika was right. There wasn't anything interesting about me except my thoughts on postmodernist theory.

Changing up the scene from a living room setting to a faux bedroom scene hadn't helped either. I still slumped like a log on the mattress.

"I've been looking at New York University, actually." I tried to sound casual. It's difficult to sound casual when you're on all fours, ass-up to the room. Even if boyshorts do hide all of your business. If I dipped my head, I could watch Audra, although she appeared upside down.

She inverted her mouth in a considering way. "Isn't that where Bishop taught?"

I winced. Even Erika had missed that detail. In truth, I had no idea where I wanted to go. I'd only settled on NYU precisely because Bishop had.

"Would it help if I suggested a few poses?" Audra said.

I nodded.

"Okay, how about you just…" She bit her lip, studying me. "I like the all fours, but try crossing your ankles. Bring your knees a little farther apart? Good. How about unbuttoning your shirt?"

It was Audra's shirt, a white collared button-down. She'd given it to me in place of my sweater set. She'd asked me to keep on the black boyshorts. I hoped the color hid the evidence of my arousal. I couldn't stop thinking about peeling her out of her top and tonguing her nipples, about pressing my face into her softness.

"Oh, I like that," Audra said and started frantically snapping shots. Without looking at me, well, looking through the lens, she said, "It's a tragic romance, isn't it?"

Lost as I was between my imaginings and this surreal scene, I had no idea what she was talking about.

"Lowell and Bishop?" She smiled. "I mean, these two great poets, the greatest of their generation, working to create new material in the wake of the postmodernists. Great intellectuals, best friends, they write each other, spend years being one another's sound board for their art, ideas, all this shit. And they couldn't have been more different. It's so obvious they're in love with each other, but just can't get it together. Can you move to the left a little? Widen your knees?"

"Like this? But it's more that they were in love with one another's *work*," I insisted. "He carried 'Armadillo' with him for years. Not to mention that he was a chronic womanizer and she was a lesbian."

"Yeah, that's good. Try relaxing your shoulders, maybe roll your hips, arch your back, like yoga, just go slow, adjust the pose, until you find what feels good and what's reaching. That's great. Dip your chin? Awesome, awesome. Maybe that was because they kept getting with people who were all wrong for them instead of the one who was right."

"You can't change your orientation," I said.

"No," Audra agreed. "Can you pull up your shirt a little? But sexuality is fluid, don't you think? It doesn't matter if you're gay or straight, you see someone attractive and you lust for them, don't you?"

She had a point. For some that was true.

"Can you take that clip out and let your hair fall over the side of your face?" I did. "Perfect. I don't know, I'm a romantic I guess. It still feels like he was the great love of her life."

"He might have been," I said, "but I think she loved her art more."

Audra smirked. "Don't we all?"

She took some final photos and let the camera down. "Okay, I think we're good. Did that feel good for you? It's awkward, I know, but you get sort of used to it. Do you think it's, well, something you'd like to do for the next few months? And before you say no..."

She hurried over to the computer with its television-sized flat monitor and plugged in her camera, dumping the pictures she'd taken. I approached slowly, wrapping the shirt tight around me, arms crossed in front of my belly, suddenly feeling exposed, like a newly peeled egg.

I was keenly aware of my bare toes curling against the cold floor.

I'd have to look at myself too? I hadn't considered that part, perhaps the most mortifying thing of all. I hated it when Erika made me fuck in front of a mirror, hated the sight of my mouth hanging open, skin flopping and sweaty. My gut clenched.

Maybe this had all been a colossal mistake. Maybe Erika was right and I should just go be a museum curator somewhere. I belonged while caring for art, not *being* art.

"Okay, check this out," Audra said.

Reluctantly, I raised my eyes to the screen.

My eyes widened.

It was me, but not me as I'd ever seen me. For one thing, I was hot. For another, see point number one.

She had me on all fours, ankles crossed, hands braced beneath my shoulders. The white shirt fell unbuttoned to either side, contrasting with the black underwear. My hair obscured my face, giving me an anonymity that felt comfortable and sexy at once. The muted white light shone in the window in front of me, contrasting with the dark all beside it. I was every woman, the ideal, softly sensual, imbued with a deep carnality that I hadn't known I possessed. Audra had plucked it from me, a musician honing her instrument. She'd taken the raw me, boyshorts and all, and made me look...well...*hot*.

Audra swiveled in the computer chair, biting her lip. "What do you think?"

I recognized, with a shock, the artist's vulnerability. She liked it, obviously. Or she wouldn't have selected this image to recruit me to the project. But she also wanted the artist's reassurance that what she'd created was good.

"Yes," I said.

Audra smiled with such enthusiasm that it made my pussy twitch. I bit back a groan when she hugged me briefly.

"Good," she said.

The portfolio grew.

Each day we worked through one or two settings, where Audra would have the room arranged when I arrived with what she thought might work, as well as an outfit laid out for me.

"I don't photograph my aunt Mildred," she said on the second day, when I showed up wearing yet another sweater set, which she cast aside with a *look*. I'd have asked what was wrong with my own clothes, but could just picture her arching her brows at me. And I already knew the answer.

They were boring.

And I had to admit, Audra's taste in clothes was amazing. Her choices for me were even better. If I had any doubts about the photos themselves, once she showed me a picture of my shoulders and back, down to the crack of my ass, a skirt at my hips, zipper undone, my elbows bent, as if she'd caught me a moment before slipping out of the garment, my doubts evaporated. From that picture, I trusted her judgment absolutely.

Slowly, images started collecting. First the initial shots she'd done, from our first day together, and the skirt picture. Then a similar back shot, my face hidden, facing the wall this time. She crouched below me as I stretched up the wall, naked, except for a pair of black tights bunched a third of the way up my ass. Then there came a series of shots, with panties clinging to the contours of my pussy; with tights stretching over the bridge of my hip bones; with my hands clutching and pressing up my bare breasts, my collarbone sharp and vulnerable.

It was hot—to see what she saw, to feel her eyes on me through the lens, her voice guiding me with subtle instruction how to move. I left our sessions increasingly flushed, feeling as though I'd been teased to the point of orgasm and denied at the last moment. My skin burned from the inside with this curbed lust.

"I'd like to try something," Audra said, considering the pictures. She worried at her lower lip with her teeth. We weren't finished for the day, but she'd grown increasingly unhappy with the day's shoot and had called a pause to reevaluate our game plan for the rest of the session. "I've been thinking." She swiveled in the chair to look at me. "This is about a journey, right? Well, there's a distinct sensuality in your photos, but I think there's an untapped element of sexuality there also, and I'd like to challenge that."

That was how Audra talked about the project. "Challenge" this, "push" that, "explore" something else.

"Our talk about Bishop the other day made me think of it, actually. How she's always so shy and appropriate, always seeking perfection. But sexual awakening is messy—I'm just thinking out loud now," she warned, "but I feel like there's something here. I want to take pictures while you masturbate. I think it's the next progression. We'll start with nudes and if you don't want to go any further, we'll stop. What do you think?"

I looked at the thumbnails on the screen. I thought of Audra, of her photographing me with my fingers in my pussy, stroking my breasts, watching me while I fantasized about her. I was far too shy to ever admit this attraction to her, so if I wanted her, this was likely the only way I would ever have her.

She'd lent me her robe for the respites we took during the shoot so I didn't have to wander around the loft half or fully naked. I twisted the belt of her robe in my hands. "Can I think about it?"

"Where do you go?" Erika asked me one day.

"What do you mean?"

"Tuesday afternoons. You've missed coffee every Tuesday for a month."

I shrugged. I hadn't told her about Audra or the photographs. It felt wrong somehow.

"Do you have a lover?"

I laughed. "When would I have time for a lover?"

It was true. As the semester progressed, the strain was beginning to take its toll on me. I slept little, ate less, reading constantly, voraciously, mentally ticking through my academic to-do list, crossing and dotting every *t* and *i* constantly...except when I was with Audra. I looked more forward to our sessions than all my other classes combined. She pushed me, challenged the ideas I held in front of me like some kind of protective talisman. Even Erika noticed the difference.

"I thought you always argued against the publication of Bishop's drafts. You said it was revealing the woman behind the curtain."

I shrugged. "I can change my mind."

She snorted. "You *don't* change your mind."

It wasn't cheating, I reasoned. Erika had kept me at arm's length our entire relationship. Besides, it wasn't that I had any intentions of sleeping with Audra. I just genuinely enjoyed her company. And her arguments made me laugh. Like how she insisted Lowell got masturbatory pleasure out of flinging his poems at the world at hurtling pace.

"No, really," she said, "think about it. He writes these things in a great creative rush and before his hands are dry from the keyboard he's got them in an envelope and off to a publisher. That's like literary masturbation."

She had me laughing so hard I could barely catch my breath.

"Well, I don't like it," Erika was saying, "I don't like playing second fiddle to whatever bohemian extracurricular bullshit you have going on. If you're with me, you're with me and I won't cater to absurdities. And what are you wearing? That shirt makes you look like a lesbian."

The shirt was Audra's.

"It looks better on you," Audra had said, waving aside my arguments when I'd protested her giving it to me.

"I *am* a lesbian," I said to Erika.

She flung her hand in dismissive wave. "You know what I mean."

I thought of Audra, of her mischievous smile as she photographed me. The way she thanked me each day when we finished shooting.

Erika had never thanked me for so much as passing a red pen.

I thought of Audra's smile and how it ignited a warm glow inside me. And how it made me immediately want to think of ways to make her smile again.

Then, to Erika, I said softly, "Maybe I don't need to be with you."

After the non-fight with Erika, I went to Audra's door and rang the bell. We hadn't done any pictures since the day she asked about shooting while I masturbated. Audra answered the door in a hastily tugged-on camisole, which she was still pulling down, and silky, clinging shorts.

"Eliza?" she said. "Is something wrong?"

It was only then I realized it was after midnight.

"Let's do it," I said, then had a moment of panic when I thought Audra might not know what I meant.

I should've known better.

"If you're uncomfortable, at any time, we can stop," Audra said.

"You're a librarian, not a model," Erika-in-my-head said.

In answer, I removed my top.

The first picture she took during this exchange showed me in profile, crouched in a yoga-like child's pose, arms by ears, hair falling out of the way over the top of my head. The light came in from behind me to make a silhouette of my breast with erect nipple. My lips were parted, eyes closed.

It was a less vulnerable pose than many of the others, and not just because this was the first one to show that I actually had a head. There was a latent sense of power in this picture, like the essence of femininity at rest.

We didn't speak. Audra had been nothing but professional and friendly during our sessions. But that didn't stop me from imagining how her skin would glide against mine, or wanting to wrap my arms around her waist, kissing her ear while we looked through photos at the end of the day. I was far too shy to ever make a move toward her. It wasn't appropriate. I wanted to be like Bishop, keep my dignity intact.

So I intended to use this session to exorcise this immense attraction I held for her, by indulging in it once and for all.

She shot me curled on my back, ankles crossed, fists clenched tight to my chest.

She shot me with my hand reaching for my pussy, a white thong stretched taut between my thighs, mouth parted, eyes closed.

I thought of how I wanted her, how hot it felt to be seen like this, to be noticed, to have her capture something about me that no one else had seen. I thought of all my fantasies from the past few months, where Audra entered the scene she'd set. She'd uncurl my crossed ankles, ease my fisted hands to the side. She'd slip the white panties down my legs. Her tongue would be on my pussy, and her fingers would plunge inside me and she'd lick and fuck me while the camera went on shooting—click by click—until my back arched off the futon, as my entire body, racked with orgasm, twisted beneath her touch; until I came so hard I lost time and woke only to her kissing me.

She shot me lying on my back on the bed, naked with a book open but obviously disregarded on one side of my abdomen, fingers lazily stroking one bare thigh, knees beginning to fall open.

She shot me with one hand at my breast, the other at my cunt, a set of vertical blinds between the camera and me, as though I was unaware of being observed.

She shot me close up, finger in my pussy, one drop of moisture dripping down the closely shaved lip.

For this, I imagined Audra lowering herself down on my face, the swollen, soft lips of her pussy full and luscious, their wine-red depths exuding an intoxicating sweet musk. I tried eating her slowly, but she would have none of it. She rode my face, thrusting shallowly with her hips, showing me how she wanted me to make her come, her juices soaking my face and running down my chin. Her breasts bounced above me, two luxuriant orbs, and when she came, she squeezed her knees around my ears, spasming above me with sharp jerks, pants and sighs that made me wet all over again.

"Good, that's good," Audra said. The camera ate up the images. "I love that look on your face." As she watched, she slowly stopped taking pictures. I rolled onto my stomach, looking at her. "What are you thinking about?"

"You," I wanted to say, but instead I rolled onto my back and began rubbing my clit. I looked directly into her eyes, something I don't usually do with people. And I began to masturbate in earnest. Audra didn't begin shooting right away. She licked her lips, transfixed by the slow circles I was making with my fingers, until she seemed to remember herself and took up the camera again.

I closed my eyes.

My pussy was wet, slick, I could feel the glide of my lips against one another between my legs. I envisioned reaching for her and her breath hitched as I touched her hair, touched my lips to hers, but she didn't resist. I embraced her, letting our bodies mold against one another as I kissed along the side of her neck. The sexy noises she made purred from the back of her throat and I felt those moans against my cunt.

I came softly, writhing against my hand, squeezing my eyes shut, all the while imagining that it was Audra bringing me, Audra stroking me, Audra holding me after.

A tear ran from the corner of one of my tightly closed eyes.

And all the while, the camera captured it all.

We shot and shot, posed and reposed, until, at last, spent,

we collapsed together on the futon. I was left shaken by my imaginings and hoped she couldn't feel me quivering beside her as we lay with our heads together, like girls at a sleepover, flicking together through the LCD images. It'd all come in such a creative rush that it left us both too drained to expend the energy of sitting at the computer.

The sheets on the bed smelled like her and twisted me inside. I felt dirty, having used her to fuel my own masturbatory fantasies. But it was done. Hopefully she had all the pictures she needed to finish her project. We'd never have to revisit this again.

I bit my lip, feeling tears prick my eyes.

Audra let out a dramatic sigh, letting her hand with the camera in it flop to the side. A moment later her other hand followed, landing on my thigh.

"That was amazing." We lay on our backs, but turned our heads so we were virtually nose to nose. "You like them, right? You're not sorry?"

I shook my head. "They're beautiful. I never...never knew I could look like that. You made me so beautiful."

"You are beautiful, luv," she said. "I only documented it."

She smiled and there was that awkward moment, when on a date we would have kissed. The moment stretched too thin and broke when Audra looked down at her hand on my thigh.

"I have an idea," she said huskily.

I was shaking when she bounced up, newly invigorated, and began setting up the camera.

The next pictures she took were just for us.

LIGHT

Destiny Moon

My hallway light burnt out so I was up on a ladder for twenty minutes trying to take out the old bulb, but I couldn't get it. It was stuck. I remembered months ago when I watched Jen do it. Her technique with a different bulb in a different lamp in a different house she used to share with my friends on the east side was a true marvel. She used masking tape and somehow managed to twist the stubborn bulb out.

So I called Jen. I only wanted to hear the theory over the phone. I may be femme, but I know how to fix things and I like doing things myself. Besides that, my last girlfriend called me a princess and I resented it, and ever since we broke up, I've tried to do everything myself.

"I'll come by later," Jen said.

"No, no. You don't have to."

"I want to."

"Well, then." I gave her directions.

Who was I to stop her? I'd never stop someone like her from

dropping by. And maybe I was secretly being a little helpless on the light bulb situation. It's not that I was clueless. I mean, everyone knows righty-tighty-lefty-loosey, I just couldn't get it to budge. And she really had been a whiz with the masking tape that other time.

Besides, she was new to the neighborhood and I was excited that we would be living closer together. There weren't that many cute butches in my vicinity.

She showed up forty-five minutes later, conveniently, minutes after I'd put a quiche into the oven. I made the pastry from scratch and baked it first to make it crispy. Then I'd sautéed mushrooms, asparagus and edamame and blended my veggies with fluffy whipped eggs and asiago. It was going to be tasty.

I opened the door. "Jen," I said, giving her a friendly hug.

"Sara." She kissed my cheek affectionately, not that it meant anything. She was just being fashionable, I was sure. "Good to see you."

"Thanks for coming."

"So, where is this pesky bulb of yours?"

I pointed straight up. It was, in fact, right in the hallway just inside my entrée.

"I brought my secret weapon." Reaching into the pocket of her leather jacket, she produced a roll of beige papery tape.

"Amazing." I clapped my hands together. "Can I watch?"

"Uh…really?"

"Well, you left an impression. You were the first person I thought of when I couldn't get it myself."

She nodded, like she'd heard that before, like she was the town expert on tricky light bulbs. "I do have a knack."

The old wooden ladder was already set up. She took off her jacket, which left her in the outfit she generally wore—a white T-shirt and jeans with black work boots. She really rocked that look. She climbed up step after creaky step and I promised I'd hold the ladder, which allowed me an excellent vantage point.

"So, how's Cole?" she enquired.

"Good, I think." I guessed she hadn't heard the news. "We broke up."

"Sorry to hear it."

"Thanks. It's okay. We'd been heading that way for a while. How's Tania?"

"That's over."

"I'm sorry."

"Don't be. We had a good few months, but then…"

"Yeah," I said to fill the silence she left when she stopped mid-sentence. There's really no need to explain the endings of things. "Sometimes you just know when the time comes."

"Exactly." Jen had taped the bulb and guided the strips of tape in a counterclockwise motion, like she was driving a car, turning left.

We were silent for a couple of minutes. I'd never invited Jen over before. This was the first time that it was just the two of us. I'd only ever seen her at parties or queer events when there were lots of people around. There was so much I didn't know about her, and suddenly my heart raced and I felt my palms get sweaty. I felt naked, like she saw right through me, like I had somehow tricked her into coming over just so I could put the moves on her or something. It wasn't true. Well, it wasn't exactly *not* true, either. I had noticed her before. Of course I had. Everyone had. But I wasn't trying to start something with her. I had thought she would just walk me through the masking tape trick over the phone and that would be that.

But here we were. Together. Not talking.

"Got it," she said, breaking the silence.

I exhaled deeply as I realized that she hadn't been talking

because she'd been concentrating on the bulb. I was, as usual, being awkward primarily in my own head.

"Awesome," I said. "You're good."

She smiled. "It was nothing." She clambered down the rickety ladder.

"Would you like to stay for quiche?" I asked. "It's in the oven right now."

"Sure." She passed me the old light bulb that had some tape on it now. "Let's make sure it works."

I flicked the switch. The light came on and for some reason I said, "Let there be light."

To my surprise she said, "And there was light."

"Whoa," I said. "Lesbians quoting Genesis."

"The beginning," she said and her eyes widened as we gazed at each other. She laughed a shy, quiet laugh as she averted her eyes and looked to the floor. "You Christian?"

"Baptized," I said. "That's about it." Then I wondered why she had asked. "You?"

"Baptist," she said.

"Cool." I nodded.

"Is it?"

"I guess," I said, remembering that I'd read an article about the Baptist church and it wasn't positive. "Want a beer?"

She looked at her watch. It was around three in the afternoon. "Sure. What the hell." She chuckled. "I'm a sinner anyway."

"Is that right?" I asked, winking.

"Hell, yeah. That's right."

"Oh, good."

We sat out on the front steps in the warmth of the September late summer. The air was balmy with notes of hyacinth and lilac in the air and only the slightest hints of fall. Because of the way

I was sitting, my dress came up far past my knees, like I was wearing a miniskirt.

When the oven buzzer sounded, I asked her to come in. She sat at my retro Formica table and watched me prepare salad while the quiche cooled. It's always better to let it sit for a while.

I found it hard to concentrate on my arugula and watercress. My gaze kept wandering to her, fixating on the way she fit in so perfectly. When I stole glances, I noticed that she was looking at me, too.

She told me she had been kicked out of Bible camp one year for kissing a girl. Then the next year her parents were called for a consultation, and by the time she was in high school, her congregation treated her as though there was something wrong with her. Seemingly to lighten the tone of what she'd just told me, she said, "It's okay. Years of therapy later, I can laugh about it and forgive."

"That's so important," I said.

"As a kid, I thought I was going to be a preacher," she said. "Like my dad."

"Wow." The song "Son of a Preacher Man" momentarily clouded my mind, and I imagined this gorgeous butch in front of me spreading the Lord's word. Now, that might just get me to go to church on Sundays. "Do you still think about it?"

She laughed a hearty belly laugh that culminated in a more serious tone. "Well, sometimes. You think I should?"

"Sure. Why not?" I chopped some red pepper into fine strips. "I mean, if you're a believer."

"I believe in 'judge not lest ye be judged' and treating people like you want to be treated."

"Pretty important," I said. "Besides, I bet you could fill those pews like nobody's business."

"You think so?" She laughed shyly.

"I'd come." I set the salad bowl down on the table and brought over the quiche. "And I never go to church. Ever."

"Well, that's mighty nice of you to say. I think I'll stick with being a courier. Guess I'd rather deliver packages than sermons."

"Fair enough."

Two hours later, I felt like I'd known her my whole life. It's incredible how whole she felt to me, how deep and multifaceted. There was so much more to her than what was visible on the surface. And how she revealed her vulnerability to me. She thanked me for listening with an open heart and told me she'd never told anyone about her religious past before, not since she moved away from her childhood town. It only added to the overwhelming sense I got that I had somehow overlooked her in these past few years of casual acquaintance. I'd seen her around. I'd noticed the way she held the door open for Tania, how she doted on her, how sweet she seemed. But I didn't really notice, didn't really see.

Until now. Now all I could do was see. She was right here in front of me, the perfect woman. My dream. The more she told me, the more I felt sure that her being here was some kind of serendipitous event. Predestined. Fated.

I told her, "I don't believe in accidents. Everything happens for a reason, like my light bulb being stuck."

"It brought me here."

I nodded.

"So we both sense what's going on here, don't we?" Her eyes met mine, and I felt like our gazes were dancing, like we'd never let each other go.

I said, "I'm not usually a fan of the old stereotypes about fast-moving lesbians. Honestly."

"Same here."

"Generally speaking, I can date casually for weeks or months. I'm not someone who falls in love and wants to move in together right away."

"Generally speaking, you said." She knew she was the exception.

I nodded. "Yeah."

I couldn't tell her that in my mind we already had children together. Maybe I'd tell her, eventually, that I saw us walking together hand in hand through life's decades all the way to the end, but not yet. On our wedding day I would tell her.

Instead, I did something decidedly more proactive. More daring. Yeah, I respected her mind, her beliefs, her life journey. But damn. Something else was going on between us and it came from deep inside.

"Come with me," I said, taking her hand.

"Anywhere," she said. But when we climbed the stairs, she asked where I was taking her.

"My bedroom," I said. "Or more specifically, my bed."

"Oh my."

"Let me tell you something," I began, but I needed to correct myself. "Actually, let me show you. They were wrong. There is nothing wrong with you. Nothing at all. You are perfect."

We entered my bedroom and I noticed she had tears in her eyes. "No one has called me perfect before."

"Well, get used to it." I turned on the bedside lamp. We'd talked so long that day had turned into night. The lamp had a very soft light. I lit the candles around my room.

She sat down on the edge of my bed. "I could definitely get used to you."

I smiled.

"Sara," she said, shaking her head from side to side as though she was in disbelief. "Sara, Sara."

I twirled around in my dress, because somehow I knew she wanted to see the way the fabric moved in the dim candlelight. She watched me closely. Paid such close attention that I felt myself blushing on the inside.

At last I climbed on top of her, straddling her.

"Do you have any idea how sexy you are?" I asked her.

She gave me a coy smile, like she knew. She put her arms around me and pulled me closer.

Our faces were incredibly close, so close I could feel the heat emanating from her. The magnetism between our lips was intense. I closed my eyes, felt our mouths collide, felt myself melt into her, like chocolate left out in the sun. I wanted nothing more than to kiss her, deeply, as though only my silent lips could communicate the closeness I felt. Words failed me and only my body could show her how gorgeous I thought she was.

Jen's hands slid stealthily up my dress. It was as though she too did not want to talk, did not want to get caught.

Quietly, we kissed and her fingers pried at the sides of my cotton panties. If this had been a date in my mind earlier, I'd have worn lace, but that would not have suited this moment. There were no accidents. As I pressed myself into her, I knew I would never be the same again.

I had seen the light.

RED VELVET CAKE

Tamsin Flowers

I love being gay, truly I do. But there's just one element to it that ticks me off. How many gay people are there in the world? Millions, right? Estimates say one in ten of the population. Some people say more. Some people say less. I say, what the hell? I'm not a statistician but by my reckoning, it ain't enough. I spend altogether too much time eyeing up girls, flirting with girls and falling for girls only to find out they don't like girls or they think they do but actually they have a boyfriend. Sometimes it's their fault. They eye me up and flirt with me. Right till we get to that first kiss moment—then they suddenly back off.

However, more often than not, it's my own fault. Or I don't see the signs. I ignore the signs. I plow on boldly, hoping against hope that they'll look at me, come to their senses and dump their boy for a happily-ever-after with this girl. Sure. I'm the queen of self-delusion. This is my schtick: I'm a lesbian, I find Girl X hot, I wouldn't find her hot if she was straight, ergo Girl X is a lesbian. For sure. Even if she doesn't realize it yet. I've kidded myself along with this routine a dozen times and now I'm sitting here, in this coffee shop, and I'm about to do it again.

Girl X is a cute little number who, in this instance, goes by the name of Flo. She's got short peroxide blond hair, a good sign, seven silver rings in one ear, a good sign, and she's wearing Doc Martens, also a good sign. Not that I mean to pre-judge or anything. I just like looking at her.

Strictly speaking, it's not my local coffee shop. There are two or three nearer to where I work, between the office and the bus stop. This one is a hundred yards beyond, in the wrong direction, but I came in here a couple of weeks back with Fin, because he rated the red velvet cake. Then I saw this girl. I had to come back, just to check if I was really taken with her and, as it turned out, I was.

I've got it bad. I'm at that stage where I could be mistaken for a stalker. I'm sitting as close by the counter as I can get, pretending I'm not staring when I am, and all the while trying to appear like my ears aren't flapping at her every conversation. So far I've learned this about her: her second name is Petersen, her father gets drunk at business conferences, her mother drives a yellow car and her brother's on the national men's gymnastics squad. There hasn't been any mention of boyfriend as far as I can make out and I haven't managed to find out where she goes drinking. If she does. But if she doesn't, she's probably not my kind of girl after all.

I get up and order another coffee. I swear this particular dalliance is going to end in the great caffeine overdose disaster. Naturally, I've timed my trip to the counter to catch Flo on her own.

"Um, another coffee, please," I say. My dry tongue sticks to the roof of my mouth, making me stumble over the words.

She looks at me blankly. Bad sign.

"What coffee?" she says. She doesn't remember my order yet? Bad sign.

"Black americano, please."

I wonder if I ought to give up now and go back to perving at Sarah Shahi in my box set of *Life*. There's no dodgy self-delusion involved in that particular crush. Just crystal-clear lust and my hand down my pants by halfway through every episode.

"I'll bring it over," she says, taking the money I hold out to her.

"Thanks." Better sign.

I go back and sit down. Is this how it's going to be forever? Long-distance stalking before I can get up the nerve to ask a girl if she's queer and if she might like to go out with me? Actually, I can't remember when I last asked a girl out. It's always this little dance around, circling closer and closer until either they knock me back or get fed up with waiting and ask me out. Or make a pass at me in the club toilets. Or cup my asscheek in their hand in a way that makes me melt inside. Yes, that did happen once— but it turned out we weren't compatible in other ways.

Flo brings my coffee over to the table and sets it down.

"Thanks." Me and my one-word vocabulary. Impressive.

Her phone rings and she digs it out of her apron pocket. A smile lights up her face as she looks at the screen. Gorgeous smile but it's not for me. It's for whoever's at the other end of the line and that, for sure, is a bad sign.

"I finish at four," she's saying. "Yeah, see you later."

I'm torturing myself over whether it's a girl or a boy she's talking to. As if it matters. If she's talking to a lover, I might as well go and start warming up the DVD player now. But of course, I don't. I text the office to say I've been held up at a meeting and then I settle in to see who turns up at four.

Two coffees and a serious case of the jitters later things go badly wrong. At five after four a guy comes in and Flo's round the front of the counter like a lightning bolt and being swept up into his arms. There's an exchange of kisses that I simply can't bear to watch. I melt away back to the office.

"Why the long face?" says Fin, from his desk opposite mine.

I shrug. I don't want to make a big deal of it. There'll be another girl in another coffee shop next week. And the week after that. And I've got my box set friends, so I can't see that I'd ever need to go back to Flo's coffee shop. If there's one thing I'm not, it's a glutton for punishment. If I know a girl's not interested, I back right off. In my experience, hanging around after a rebuff doesn't do anyone any favors.

So now I'm busy forgetting all about Flo or Mo or whatever her damned name was. Moving on. There's a girl I see on the bus regularly who I think is cute. And there's a lifeguard I like to perv when I take my niece swimming once a week. I practice drowning in the bathtub and life's a blast. I get a lot of work done.

It takes about three weeks before Fin needs another red velvet cake hit. I'm not wild about the idea but I think I'm out of trouble. Flo-Mo might have moved on by now anyway—in my experience girls who work in coffee bars generally have ants in their pants and it's the ultimate in transferable job skill. So I'm not expecting to see her.

But she's there all right, looking just the same, and my heart skips a little beat just to let me know that I haven't gotten over her. I haven't forgotten her and I know perfectly well her name's Flo, not Mo or Jo. Fin goes up to the counter to order while I find us a table as far away from my girl as possible. I pick the chair facing out the window so I don't have to pretend I'm not staring at her. I resolutely watch the traffic going by on the street while I wait for Fin to return with my coffee fix and his cake. But when he comes back he's just got two cups of coffee.

"Don't tell me they're out of red velvet cake?" I say. "We could have had the coffee to go."

He shakes his head. "No, no, it's coming."

I take a sip of my coffee, all nonchalance, just enjoying a break with a friend. No one needs to know my stomach's churning and the coffee tastes like dead cigarette ash in my mouth.

The plate with the red velvet cake makes a cracking sound on the glass tabletop, and I start.

"You've got a nerve, coming back here," hisses a voice in my ear.

I look round to see Flo's back receding toward the counter.

"Jesus, Carrie, did you and Flo have a thing?" says Fin, his eyebrows disappearing under his heavy side-swept bangs.

"You know her?"

"Yeah." Of course he did. "That's why I brought you here in the first place—I thought she might be your type."

"Um, Fin, I seem to remember we came here so you could pig out on red velvet cake."

"Well, yeah, it's good here. But…"

"She's so not my type, Fin. She's got a guy."

Fin laughs and shakes his head. "Nuh-uh. I totally know she's queer."

"Anyway, nothing happened and I don't know why she said that." I'm getting hot and bothered, and gulping down my scalding coffee doesn't help.

"She's just gone out for a smoke, so why don't you go ask her?"

"No way."

"Then you'll never know."

I blink.

"Anyone can see there's something going down here. But you're happy with not knowing?"

"Yup."

I sit and drink my coffee, quite content with not knowing.

Yeah, right. I'm out through the back door like greased lightning. There's a small paved yard at the back of the coffee shop, crowded with bins, beyond which an open gate leads out into the rear parking lot. Flo isn't cozying up to the garbage so I go through the gateway to look for her.

I don't have to go far. She's leaning on the bonnet of a yellow Honda, taking short, sharp puffs on a cigarette. She glowers when she sees me.

"What do you want?" she says, exhaling a cloud of smoke.

I step closer and breathe it in, wishing I was still a smoker. "What did you mean in there? I've got a nerve?"

"Like I said, you've got a nerve, coming back here."

I shake my head. "I don't get it."

She nods hers. "Really? You really don't get why I might not want to see you back here?"

This is like ping-pong.

"No." I step up closer still and square my shoulders, ready for a fight.

She flicks ash, aiming at my shoe. She's a good shot. She takes a long, deep drag and then crushes the butt with her foot. When she exhales in my face, I want to kiss her.

"You come in, day after day. Your eyes follow me round the room like a sick puppy. You give off vibes. And then, when you've reeled me in and got me jonesing for you, you fucking disappear. Poof!" She snaps her fingers up near my face. "Gone."

I chew on the inside of my cheek, trying to think of something to say.

"What was that all about?" She sounds angry and hurt.

I swallow. "That boy," I say. "There was a boy. I thought…"

"You thought. That was my brother."

She's already heading back toward the gate when I slam her up against the wall.

"So I got it wrong. I'm sorry."

She's panting and my heart's pounding hard and fast. She stares up at me, wide-eyed—and for me this becomes the decision point, the do-or-die moment. I could step back with another apology and leave, or I can step forward and take her mouth. I'm scared. Paralyzed.

"Flo…"

Disappointment floods her features. As she tries to push past me to leave, I put my hands on her shoulders and my lips on her mouth. I kiss her the way I should have kissed her the first day I saw her in the coffee shop. Sure, I'm tentative at first, but when I glance up her eyes tell me yes and the push of her body against mine tells me to get on with it. I kiss her harder and push my tongue into her mouth. She tastes of the cigarette she's just smoked and that's fine by me. It's a kiss I don't want to surface from and my body pushes back against hers, setting off a succession of little starbursts that run from my cunt up to my sternum.

Her hand goes to my breast and then, not content with feeling it through the fabric, she yanks up my T-shirt to touch the bare flesh. Her fingers are cool and smooth, and my nipple responds by standing to attention. She pulls her mouth away from mine and here I am, standing in a public parking lot, having my breast suckled by the girl of my dreams. My breath catches in my throat and my legs liquefy. I run my fingers through her short hair and moan.

"Come with me," she says. Her voice carries a tremor that

I want to bottle so I can listen to it later. Over and over again. "Come with me. Come with me."

I follow her back through the gate, heavy limbed, wondering where she's taking me. Not back to Fin and his red velvet cake and my coffee, please god. I reach out to touch her ass and she slows down halfway across the yard to take my caress. She's wearing denim shorts, and by dropping my hand a bit lower I'm able to make contact with the smooth skin at the top of her thigh.

"Come on," she says. She sounds breathy.

We go inside, but instead of turning left to the front of the shop, Flo leads me down a passage to the right. She pulls a bunch of keys from her pocket and unlocks a door, disappearing inside. The storeroom. I blink in the half dark and see shelves stacked with catering size bags of coffee beans, boxes of tea, bags of sugar and cartons of candy. Flo shuts the door behind us and wastes no time in pulling off her tank.

I stand staring. She has magnificent breasts. Not big but beautifully spherical with dark, bullet-shaped nipples that I immediately want to stretch and pull with my teeth. I do that, pushing her down onto a laundry bag as I catch one of them in my mouth. She gives a soft yelp, struggles out of her shorts underneath me and turns her attention to my jeans. I kick off my sneakers and leave her to it while I concentrate on mauling her breasts. The skin's silken and salty, puckering tighter as my tongue traces a circle around one of the hard nubs.

Her fingers dive into my panties and tug them down around my thighs and then both hands go on an exploration of what she's uncovered. She strokes my ass and cups my front. Fingers run along each side of my lips and then up between them. Of course, I'm wet and she finds her way inside as smoothly and sleekly as an otter slipping into a stream. Two fingers push upward, making me bite down on her nipple as sensation floods me. She gasps and then giggles, pushing me down so I'm lying next to her. She pulls her breast from my mouth and straddles me, both of us buck naked now, crotch to crotch.

I moan and she puts a finger to my lips. I lick it and it tastes of me. But I want a taste of her, so I reach between her legs. The folds of flesh part for me as she splays her legs wider and I stroke the thin strip of dark curls that beckon me down. Her hips grind against mine as my fingers breach her outer walls and a warm flood runs down my hand as I push up inside. So soft, so yielding, so damn hot I can hardly breathe.

I pull my fingers out for a quick taste but her pained whimper tells me she needs them back and I immediately reenter, pushing higher and harder, fucking her with my hand until she moves against me in the same rhythm. But my need to taste her overwhelms me, so I snatch my fingers away and put both hands on her hips. I pull her forward, bringing her cunt up to my face, breathing in the musky smell of her as my tongue steals out to find what it needs.

She tastes so good, so sweet, that I could drink her all day long. Nectar flows from the hot, dark crevasse between her legs, a river of desire that I want to immerse myself in as fully as I can. I suck her clit into my mouth and then go back to finger-fucking her and it only takes a minute to make her come. The rings of muscle inside her cunt spasm against my fingers as her back arches above me—the muffled moan from her throat should really be a scream. She grabs at my hair, pushing my face hard against her groin, and I work her clit with my tongue until she has to pull me away.

Both panting, we lie back on the laundry bag. She dips a hand between my legs and I open up to her touch. Deft fingers know what they're doing, playing my clit and sliding in and out of me with a quickening pulse. She kisses my mouth and I surrender completely to the fires she's conjuring inside me, sliding into my orgasm and falling deep. When the flames die down and I open my eyes, I'm cradled in her arms and she's looking down at me with wide, dark eyes.

"I knew I wanted you the first time you came in," she whispers in my ear, "but I thought you were with that guy."

"He came for the red velvet cake and I came for you."

She laughs.

"Yes, you did," she says. "You came for me."

UNEXPECTED BLISS

Gun Brooke

It was easy to become hypnotized while sitting in a meeting led by Magdalena Cole. Personal assistant Pam Garner was often bored by the subject, but was always mesmerized by her boss.

Magdalena, always striking with her short, black hair, kept in a no-frills hairdo reaching her earlobes, commanded the meetings, whether they were small staff conferences or large stockholder gatherings. Using her light blue eyes together with her soft-spoken voice and venomous choice of words, she kept her audience riveted. She could purr like a kitten and still come across like a cobra ready to strike at some unsuspecting minion without warning. Pam knew all about Magdalena's methods. Neutral looks were best. Smiles usually a warning if they were too toothy, hinting at barracuda. Then her fiery eyes, which could drill into yours. Oh boy, that was when employees, her peers and even burly stockholders became suicidal within seconds.

It still boggled Pam's mind that nobody seemed to have picked up on the rest of Magdalena's mood indicators. Her voice had different qualities, and yes, they were subtle, but so easily distinguishable. The purr could be soft, like a fleece blanket wrapping around you on a winter evening, that Pam could listen to, no matter what was actually said, for the longest time. Then the purr could have a sharp hiss to it, as if the fangs were coming out, the venom gathering and, sure enough, Magdalena would say something cutting and sarcastic.

When she talked to her sons, she sounded protective and gentle. Before her husband filed for divorce, she had a special tone for him as well, apologetic, tired, slightly exasperated. Pam thought it was the closest to people-pleasing that Magdalena would most likely ever get. That tone always used to make Pam cringe. Thankfully, after the divorce proceedings commenced, Pam never heard it again.

When Magdalena talked to Manon Belmont or any other members of the board, her voice was definitely neutral. None of the lethal hissing, no purring, just straight on matter-of-fact, and with Ms. Belmont, friendly. When it came to people Magdalena loathed, Pam thought it might be possible to measure the temperature change when Magdalena's voice dropped to an icy register. It was a miracle the recipient's nose and earlobes didn't sustain permanent frostbite.

As always, Pam took copious notes automatically while Magdalena and the others around the table brainstormed the next benefit gala. And as always, Pam was distracted by her boss's hands. Pale, soft looking and elegant, they moved to emphasize her words. Magdalena normally kept her nails blunt and just slightly longer than her fingertips, with a perfectly executed French manicure. Like her signature hoop earrings, she wore large, statement rings on her fingers. Especially since she stopped wearing her engagement and wedding rings, she had favored bold custom jewelry.

Pam frowned. Something was not right. Or at least, something about Magdalena's hands was not the same as usual. Magdalena wore a chunky silver ring on her left ring finger and she kept pushing at it, which in itself was no big deal, but the thing was, she was trying to conceal doing it. And then there was the slight grimace that flickered over her face every now and then. If Pam hadn't known any better, she would've thought it was a sign of Magdalena being in pain.

After the meeting, Magdalena hurried into her private restroom, only to emerge ten minutes later, looking furious. Pam had flipped her blond ponytail over her shoulder to her back and started typing out the notes from the meeting, but she couldn't take her eyes from the stark beauty of a wrath-filled Magdalena.

Knowing full well she was literally poking the lioness, she said, "Something wrong, Magdalena? Can I help?"

"Unless you forgot to write field surgeon on your résumé, I doubt it." Magdalena sat down at her desk, cradling her left hand.

Worried now, as she usually saw Magdalena as invincible—well, except for the time in Paris when she'd found her wiping tears in her hotel room after Stephen announced he wanted a divorce—Pam braved the threshold to Magdalena's office. "You look like you're in pain. Please, isn't there anything I can do?"

Magdalena scowled at Pam, but there was no genuine fire in her gaze. "Do we have a toolbox somewhere on this floor?"

Toolbox? Pam knew she was expected to handle the unexpected, but she would never have guessed that entailed playing carpenter or plumber. Risking even more by asking questions, which, though not forbidden, wasn't recommended, she said, "I think maintenance has a storage room somewhere at the other end of the corridor. Why?"

"If you're going to help me, you'll need some strong cutters."

Magdalena held up her hand. "I can't get it off." The last sentence was uttered with total disgust and slight panic. The former was a familiar tone; the second, not so much.

Pam bent over Magdalena's desk and looked in horror at a very swollen, pink-purple ring finger. Clearly the huge ring would not slide off.

"God, Magdalena. I'll go find the toolbox. I'll hurry."

"You do that." Magdalena leaned back and closed her eyes.

As it turned out, Pam didn't have to look. An electrician was working outside the office and his toolbox was sitting right there. After assuring him he'd get the wire cutter back ASAP, she ran back to Magdalena's office, where she found Magdalena standing by the window, cradling her hand while chewing on her lower lip.

"I have the cutter. Do you want to do it here...or?" Pam motioned for Magdalena's restroom.

"The restroom." Magdalena strode off, and Pam scrambled after her.

The restroom smelled of Magdalena's perfume, an amazingly enticing scent of fresh flowers, fruit, sandalwood...and something else, something sweet. Magdalena stood by the sink, looking down at the offending ring with her lips pursed.

"Why don't you sit down?" Pam could tell she would have to take temporary command here. She pointed at the small makeup table. "There, on the stool? I'll just clean this a little bit, even if it is in pretty good shape."

Running the faucet, Pam felt rather silly using the expensive hand soap to clean a crude tool, but there was no way she'd let it near Magdalena's skin without at least a quick washing first. Turning to Magdalena, she realized she would have to kneel next to her boss in order not to get in her own light. Not about to hurt her knees on the tile floor, she tossed two folded towels next to the stool and knelt.

A muted gasp from Magdalena made Pam look up. Magdalena's formerly pale cheeks were suddenly pink and her pupils dilated.

"Don't worry. I've done this before." Trying for a reassuring smile, Pam patted Magdalena's knee before she realized what she was doing. *Oh, boy, keep this up and I'll be out of a job.*

"Then proceed." Magdalena held out her hand.

Pam took her hand and all her synapses fired at once. Just holding Magdalena's hand ignited so many sensations, it was ridiculous. If she had ever wondered what the true nature of her feelings for Magdalena was, it was no longer a mystery. As surely as she knew the sun set in the west, she realized she'd fallen in love with Magdalena Cole without meaning to. This was not good news. It was a one-way street to heartache.

Forcing herself to focus on the offending ring, Pam examined it closely. She wondered how long Magdalena had struggled to get it off, as it had nearly chafed the skin off in two places. "I think I'll try to cut it as close to the—"

"Just do it."

"All right. It will hurt, but I'll try to—"

"Pamela."

Right. Shut up and do it. Pam took a deep breath as she pushed one of the blades of the cutter between Magdalena's sore finger and the ring. Magdalena's soft moan proved how much it hurt. Squeezing the tool's handle slowly, Pam could still not prevent it from jumping as the blades snapped through the ring.

"Ah!" Magdalena gripped Pam's shoulder tightly and closed her eyes hard. Tears clung to her lashes.

"Halfway there." Pam pulled another tool from the pocket in her pants. "This tool will expand—oh, wow, don't set my hair on fire, Magdalena. I'm hurrying."

She pushed the other tool between the cut edges and pried the ring open, enlarging it gradually until she could slide it off. "You better wash your hands and perhaps have Belmont's nurse—"

"No. I'll wash and you may put some Band-Aids on it." Magdalena spoke huskily as she pivoted and washed her hands while still sitting on the stool. "You surprise me, Pamela. I never knew you'd handle a personal crisis of mine this well. And expediently." She wiped her hands on a clean towel and pointed at a shelf. "First aid kit."

Pam pulled out two Band-Aids and affixed them to Magdalena's finger. Reluctantly she let go of the slender hand. "There. You need to keep it elevated a bit."

"Yes. Well." Magdalena merely sat there, scanning Pam's face.

Pam couldn't move. Magdalena's gaze was a caress against her cheeks, as frightening as it was wonderful. The ice blue in Magdalena's eyes was not cold anymore. Instead her eyes radiated warmth—or was it heat?—and Pam wanted to stay in this wondrous state forever, but of course that was impossible.

"A-anything else I can do for you, Magdalena?"

"A loaded question right now, don't you agree?" Magdalena's lids lowered slowly and rose again.

"Loaded?" Pam sucked her lower lip between her teeth.

"You sit there, kneeling at my feet, and ask if there's anything else you can do for me. You hold my hand so tenderly and tend to me as if I were made of glass—as if I was somehow incredibly valuable. It can be misconstrued. It can be interpreted as something less than innocent."

Pam couldn't breathe normally. How transparent had she been that Magdalena spoke such impossible words? Was she about to ridicule her, fire her, blacklist her? "Magdalena..."

Magdalena cupped Pam's cheek. "Your eyes will be your

downfall if you don't learn to hide your thoughts better, Pamela. I can read you very well, and if I can, so can others. Still, I admit I hope you don't look at anyone else this exact way. That would be most upsetting."

She ran her thumbs under Pam's eyes, and only then did Pam realize she was crying a little, trembling under Magdalena's gentle touch. Afraid to ask, Pam still had to know.

"How...what do you mean, upsetting?"

"I simply wouldn't like it if you looked at someone else the way you look at me. As if you really care. And sometimes as if you might pounce on me."

Pam could've sworn her heart stopped at Magdalena's incredible words. "Pounce?"

"Do you deny desiring me, Pamela?" Magdalena whispered. "I've seen it in your eyes, on your face, for quite some time." She laced her fingers through Pam's hair. "Your beautiful chocolate brown eyes, they melt when I look at you. Makes me wonder how it feels for you."

"Right now? I'm ready to faint."

Magdalena chuckled and some of Pam's tension drained away. She relaxed as Magdalena caressed her hair, down her neck, then cupped her shoulders.

"I do care, Magdalena. I hope it doesn't make you uncomfortable. I never intended for you to know."

"I'm not uncomfortable." Magdalena sounded taken aback. "And though I can understand why you'd err on the side of caution, I'm...I'm glad I know."

Whoa! How could this be happening? If Magdalena only knew how she felt, how much she wanted her, she might throw her out for sure. Shaken, Pam pulled away, needing to put some distance between herself and Magdalena, but Magdalena slid off the chair and knelt next to her, their eyes now at the same level.

Pam lost what little breath she had left and just stared. Magdalena slowly wrapped her arms around Pam's shoulders. "Am I wrong to think kissing you would be welcome?" She tilted her head just so. "May I, Pamela?"

Shivering in Magdalena's arms—*Magdalena's arms*—Pam only nodded. Her voice was way beyond malfunctioning. When Magdalena leaned closer, Pam closed her eyes, only to snap them open again, not wanting to miss a thing. Still, when Magdalena's lips pressed against hers, she couldn't keep eyes open. Closing them, she inhaled Magdalena's scent and hugged Magdalena tighter. If this was the only time she'd be allowed to experience this with Magdalena, she'd make the most of it.

Magdalena moaned into the kiss and pushed both hands into Pam's hair, lifting her mouth away only enough to change the angle of the kiss. She ran the tip of her tongue along Pam's lower lip and Pam opened to her, wanting so badly to deepen the kiss and taste her. Carefully, Pam met the tip of Magdalena's tongue with hers. Her thighs quivered and she clung to Magdalena, reveling in the sweetness of her.

"Pamela," Magdalena murmured against her lips. "My god, this...I didn't expect this."

Unable to form words, Pam abandoned all caution and wrapped her fingers in Magdalena's hair, a silky soft anchor.

"I didn't expect you to penetrate all my defenses." Magdalena pulled back and frowned. "I never thought I'd fall head over heels for a girl half my age on the floor of a Belmont loo."

Her normally dormant British accent broke through and Pam couldn't help herself. Leaning her forehead against Magdalena's shoulder, she laughed uncontrollably.

"Really, Pamela. I fail to see the humor—"

"Come on, Magdalena. The way you said 'loo'...with such disdain. It was funny." Pamela could tell Magdalena wasn't really annoyed. She wore that tiny smirk showing she was seconds away from a real smile.

"I suppose." And there it came, a broad, blinding and rare smile.

Pam had never seen anything more beautiful than Magdalena Cole smiling happily. She just had to kiss the corners of that smile. While she was at it, she continued down Magdalena's neck and finished with a long, smoldering kiss to the indentation below Magdalena's neck. "You're right. I do desire you, Magdalena. I can't help it any more than I can help the reason I desire you. Now that you know, will you allow me to prove that I can still work for you?"

"For the time being." Magdalena's cheeks flushed with color and her eyes glowed. "If this...this desire we are experiencing continues and we decide we want something, um, more permanent, you can't stay on."

"Oh." Pam's brain had nearly imploded at the words *desire we are experiencing* and her heart nearly exploded when Magdalena said *something more permanent*.

"By then you'll have earned your right to receive a very satisfactory letter of recommendation."

"Ah. Thank you."

"Don't thank me yet. You may still screw things up." Her expression was deadpan but her tone playful. A new tone, one Pam liked.

"I won't, Magdalena." Pam kissed her. "I won't."

Cupping Pam's cheeks, Magdalena's expression softened. "Workwise, I'll string you up if you do, but in private, that is another matter. Regardless of my reputation, and the testimony of my ex-husband, I don't use people I love. I don't deliberately take them for granted or mistreat them. Nor do I pass judgment and show them the door if they should happen to screw up."

Running her fingertips along Magdalena's cheek, Pam smiled gently. "Did you say people you love?"

Blushing, Magdalena closed her eyes briefly. "I did, didn't I?"

"I think you did."

"Am I to understand that you love me, Pamela?"

"Yes," Pam said, taking the leap, somehow knowing it was necessary that she do so. Pam didn't wait for Magdalena to reply, but stood and held out her hand.

Magdalena took it and rose to her feet with her usual elegance. She checked her watch. "Might I suggest you come home with me? We can have dinner together and discuss this unforeseen turn of events."

Pam smiled, the tenderness welling in her heart nearly choking off her words. "Only you would call making out on the bathroom floor an unforeseen turn of events. And yes, I would love to have dinner with you."

"Well." Magdalena kissed Pam firmly. "Let's get our coats. I can't wait to have you alone."

Pam turned to leave, but a slender hand cupped her neck.

"Why can't I keep my hands off you, Pamela?" Magdalena murmured. "It's as if they have a life and mind of their own when you're around."

"I don't mind. I love your hands." Pam kissed Magdalena's tempting lips. "And this unforeseen turn of events has made me hungry."

Magdalena gave that genuine smile again. "You do look famished."

Pam laughed again. Famished was one word for how she felt about this woman. She could think of many, many more.

WATERFALL

LT Masters

The sun wasn't quite up yet and I shouldn't have been either. I stared at Brad, studying his breathing pattern. He was definitely asleep. I found my hiking boots, tugged them on, crawled out of the tent and stretched. Someone five foot nine isn't meant to sleep in a five-foot tent, and I still couldn't believe I was in the middle of nowhere, sleeping on the ground. No one would ever believe "Ms. Professional" would be doing the things I had the past two days. No restroom, no shower, what was I thinking? I always had trouble saying no to Brad, who was on a mission to rescue me from the dull routine of the big city, something he detested but I was just fine with. I let him convince me to spend the weekend with him in the mountains. Little did I know spending the weekend with him also included mosquitoes, ticks, fleas and his ex-girlfriend, who happened to be "Ms. Wilderness." When she started talking about the exact right way to build a fire from dry needles and dung or something, I decided to put pinecones in her sleeping bag.

I rifled through my bag and scribbled a quick note, which I left on the cooler under a roll of dew-moistened toilet paper. Then I grabbed my backpack and started walking down the trail. Everyone in the campsite was still asleep, and it would be at least an hour before anyone realized I was gone. If I moved quickly, within the hour I could hitch a ride back to town at the trailhead. I rolled up the sleeves on my red flannel shirt and noticed my nails. Damn it, the nice work that was done two days prior wasn't at all evident in the chipped, flaking red varnish. Nope. Time to go. He could enjoy getting dirty with his ex, whose nails weren't a concern for her.

I don't recall how long I walked, but the trail seemed quite a lot longer than it had two days before. I rested against a pine tree to catch my breath. Beads of perspiration were already forming on my neck. I pulled my hair up and secured it with a rubber band and thought of my shower at home and how good it would feel. Frustrated, tired, thirsty and sick of the great outdoors, I sat down on a rock with my face in my hands and cried. I wasn't usually the damsel-in-distress type, but it occurred to me that if I was lost, they wouldn't know how to find me. I closed my eyes and tried to calm down. Deep breathing helped me relax and I dozed off. A sharp noise startled me awake. I jumped up and smacked my head against a low-hanging branch and fell to the ground with a thud. I lay there stunned, unwilling to move as the world spun far too fast and bile rose in the back of my throat. Pain in my ankle shot up my leg, adding to the nausea-inducing spinning. The light turned to a pinprick and then went out.

When I woke, I opened my eyes only to be greeted by the deep blue sky above me. I attempted to sit up but strong hands were on my arms, holding me down.

"Take it easy," a woman said. "You're okay."

Frightened, I lay still as she dabbed a cold cloth on my forehead and face.

"Do you feel all right?" she asked.

I attempted to speak but couldn't. My throat was so dry and tight all I managed was a squeak.

"Here," she said, lifting her canteen from around her neck. "I bet you could use some water. Are you hurt anywhere?"

I moved a bit and flinched with pain. "My ankle. And my head feels worse than a tequila hangover."

Immediately she began unlacing my hiking boot.

"Yep," she said, turning my ankle in her hands, "you've twisted it good. Got some major swelling here. Better get some ice on it." She opened her backpack and removed an ice pack from a stocked first aid kit.

"Looks like you're prepared." I was impressed with the contents, which included everything from ammonia inhalants to zoo animal crackers.

She nodded. "You never know what's lurking in these woods. Or who you'll find passed out under a tree. I hike here a lot." She pressed the pack against my ankle and I jumped from the cold.

She shifted her weight to sit cross-legged, my foot resting in her lap. "Are you comfortable? Hopefully we can get this swelling down so you can walk."

I figured I should ask her questions, do the small-talk thing. Hell, introduce myself and find out who she was. But instead I closed my eyes again. At least I wasn't alone, and this woman clearly knew what she was doing. She'd get me back to civilization and a hot shower in no time. I drifted to sleep.

When I woke I was alone. The sun had disappeared behind the trees and shadows were beginning to blanket the forest. I shivered, unsure if it was from the chill or fear. I sat up and glanced around. Where was the woman? Had it all been a dream? Was I really alone? In my panic I attempted to stand, but when I did the pain in my ankle forced me to cry out.

"Don't do that!" Within seconds she was beside me, grasping my elbow. "Don't put your weight on it."

I leaned on her for support. Her short black hair was damp and her skin against my arm was cool and clammy. "You're wet," I whispered. There was something intense and ready about her, like an animal in the wild. I was suddenly very aware of just how attractive she was.

She stared down at me, silent.

I felt lost, consumed by the blue depths of her eyes, and my body swayed toward her. She grabbed me tight and lowered me back to the ground. Her thigh brushed against mine. The electricity sparked by the contact was just fear and a desire not to be left alone. That was all.

"You're in no condition to walk." She sat back on her heels. "And that's a nasty bump on your head. Based on the way you were out, I'm thinking concussion. Guess we'll have to stay here tonight."

I started to protest but decided it was pointless. What was I going to do? Hobble into the woods and get lost again?

"My camp isn't far," she continued. "I'll go get some things and be back shortly."

"No! Don't leave me here." My pride fled at the thought of being alone, and I didn't even care that my voice had gone octaves higher than an opera singer's.

She glanced at me and smiled. "Not a woman of the woods, huh?"

I shook my head. "Kinda obvious, isn't it?"

"Well," she said, looking up and down my body in a way

that made me flush, "hiking alone without water is a dead give-away."

I felt the color rise to my face and thought I should tell her about Brad and how much I hated the woods but decided against it. If she knew I had friends out there, she might take me back to them. And for some reason, I really didn't want to leave her just yet.

She produced a sandwich and an apple from her backpack and shared it with me. When we had finished, she stood and brushed herself off. I couldn't help but notice how fit she was, how lithe and lean. I was tall, but she was even taller. I looked at her face and was mortified when I realized she'd been watching me stare at her body.

She grinned. "I'll be gone half an hour, maybe an hour, tops. I need to at least grab something to sleep on. My camp isn't far, but your ankle is still way too swollen for you to walk on it. So we'll have to stay here. I'm Jordan, by the way."

"Claire."

She waved as she loped off into the woods and I stayed quiet, knowing that if I opened my mouth I'd beg her not to leave again, and I knew she was right. The last thing I wanted to do was sleep totally uncovered in the open air, which was beginning to feel strangely claustrophobic. *What the hell is wrong with me? Who gets hot for a stranger when they're lost and alone in a forest? Me, evidently.* She wasn't gone long, but I still breathed easier when she got back.

She unrolled her sleeping bag. "I only have one, but lucky for us, it's a double." She cleared the ground of all the sticks and stones.

I was a bit nervous about sharing a sleeping bag with a stranger, but nonetheless I was thankful I wasn't alone.

Jordan removed her boots, socks and shirt. I looked away as

she released her belt and unbuttoned her cargo shorts.

"Okay, now for you."

Startled, I glanced at her. She was standing in front of me in her sports bra and teddy-bear-covered boxer shorts. I couldn't help but laugh.

"Hey," she said, "it's my roughing-it attire. You shouldn't sleep in the clothes you're wearing during the day if you can help it. That way you've got dry clothes to put on in the morning."

I extended my arms, figuring the wood nymph would know what she was talking about. She pulled me up and I stumbled forward against her. Our bodies were in full contact, her breasts pressed firmly against mine, our thighs touching. Her fingertips grazed my buttcheek. Immediately I pulled away.

"Sorry," I muttered, still leaning on her for support but trying to put some distance between us. I'd never in my life been so flustered in another woman's proximity.

She smiled as though she knew what I was thinking. "What assortment of these clothes do we need to get rid of?"

Since I wasn't wearing a bra, the T-shirt was definitely staying on. I untied the flannel shirt around my waist and let it fall to the ground. "This, I guess. And my shorts…" I wobbled as I shifted my balance to undo my shorts and she stopped me.

"Brace yourself on my shoulder." She swiftly unhooked my belt and unbuttoned my shorts and they fell around my ankles. She pulled them away, set them to the side, and lowered her gaze to my black thong. "Much better. You'll be more comfortable now."

Her voice was deep, throaty. Without warning she grabbed my T-shirt and tugged it upward. I felt my arms go up and the shirt slide over my head. It was as though I had no mind of my own, no willpower. I stood bathed in the dusky sunset light, my breasts exposed, my nipples hard. What was happening to me? Who was this woman? She stared at my breasts, her own breathing ragged. My body ached for her touch and I had a sudden longing to feel her mouth on my nipples, her hands roaming my body. *I'm insane. Certifiably. Maybe I hit my head harder than I thought, and this is all a really good dream.*

She dragged her hands through her hair and looked away. There was a long moment of silence between us before she turned back to me with a tight smile and wrapped her arm around my waist. "Come on, let's get you settled in."

She checked my ankle again. Her touch was like fire on my skin. "You'll be better by morning, the swelling's going down already."

We settled down back to back in the sleeping bag and, exhausted, I slept surprisingly well. When I opened my eyes, she was the first thing I saw, lying on her side facing me, sleeping peacefully. I studied her rugged features: dark eyebrows, straight sharp nose, chiseled jawline and beautiful soft lips. A lock of her hair fell across her forehead. I brushed it aside with my fingertips.

"Good morning." She yawned, opening her eyes. "Feeling okay?"

I nodded, words escaping me in the face of her stunning good looks, even after a night spent sleeping outside on the ground. I probably looked like I'd been dragged through a hedge backward.

She propped herself up on her elbow, her head resting on the palm of her hand. "I always go for a swim first thing in the morning. Wanna join me? The water would be good for your ankle."

She tossed me my T-shirt, helped me to my feet and knelt down to inspect my ankle. It was still tender but nothing like the day before. "You should be able to walk today as long as it's not too far."

Seeing her in front of me on her knees was having the kind of effect I wouldn't want her to see. I took a step back, hoping that she hadn't noticed the wet spot forming in my panties. The heat in her eyes told me she had definitely noticed. I looked away and motioned toward the river. I leaned on her and hobbled to the river. Seeing the waterfall up close in the early morning light was mesmerizing, like something out of a fantasy movie. The water spilled over the edge of massive boulders, crashing into the pool below. The rocks, the crystal-blue water. It was…

"Breathtaking, huh? Come on," she said, grabbing my hand, pulling me forward. "Let's swim."

"I can't," I said. "No swimsuit."

She released my hand and laughed as she pulled her sports bra off. "No need."

My mouth fell open as she stripped off her clothes and dove into the water. Her body was so beautiful, muscular and golden brown. I watched as she swam to the pool beneath the waterfall.

"Hurry," she yelled, waving to me.

Remembering that I hadn't experienced anything similar to a shower in three days, I quickly stripped off the T-shirt and thong and joined her in the water. She'd already seen me topless. Hell, she'd spent the night in the same sleeping bag with me in nothing but my thong. At least in the water I'd be submerged.

The icy-cold water made me gasp but it soothed my aching body as I swam to meet her, and I felt refreshed.

"This is the first time I've been here with someone."

"Really?" I said. "What's so special about this place?"

"Let me show you." She swam to where the water was falling into the pool.

I swam closely behind her, and when she disappeared under the surface I did too. The water was pounding into the pool, creating a magical sea of bubbles underwater. I swam fast to keep up with her, trying not to stare at the long, shapely legs or firm ass in front of me. Within seconds we surfaced.

She lifted herself from the water and leaned over to help me.

"What is this place?" I asked.

"Nature's canvas."

I stood in awe, trembling, hugging myself. We were in a massive cave behind the waterfall, shut away from the outside world. Glimmers of sharp sunlight slipped through the cascading water, illuminating and reflecting off the stone walls. On the other side of the waterfall the water drained from the pool, splashing over the rocks, creating a small stream that lazily cut its way down the mountainside. The rocks we stood on were polished smooth and I slipped a little as I turned to look around.

"Careful," she teased, "don't aggravate your injury."

Playfully she grabbed my hands, lacing her fingers between mine. Dangerously close, I attempted to move away from her, but my back was pressed firm against the cold stone wall. She kept hold of my hand and moved with me. I shivered from the chill of the stones and the excitement of her warm body pressed against mine.

"Are you scared?" She gazed at me, her eyes hungry and full of desire.

"No," I lied.

She lowered her gaze to my erect nipples pressed firmly against her breasts. My fleshy pale 38Cs pushed flat against her much smaller breasts and her bronzed, muscular chest made an interesting sight. The contrast was…sexy. Hot. Erotic.

"May I?" she murmured.

I swallowed against the huge lump in my throat. What would life on the other side of the waterfall be like if I said yes? What was it like before? Why could I not recall?

Obviously sensing my hesitation, she stepped away.

Panic pulsed through me, my decision made. I pulled her back.

She lowered her head and took my right nipple into her mouth.

I gasped, my knees weak as pure lust raced through me and settled between my legs.

She positioned a leg between mine and pressed her hips firmly against me. As she licked and sucked my nipple, my body arched. Need and desire roared through me. I twisted and moaned, my neglected breast aching for the pleasure of her mouth. Arousal launched a waterfall between my legs to rival the one beside us. She abandoned my breast and stepped back to study the sticky spot on her leg.

My face flushed with heat and I looked away.

"Don't be embarrassed." She dipped her forefinger in it, traced it across her top lip, then slowly licked it off. "You're delicious."

My heartbeat quickened as she lowered herself until she was on her knees, eye level with my throbbing sex. When she leaned forward I spread my legs, inviting her. Slowly she licked my inner thighs in long smooth strokes until she removed all my wetness.

I pressed my palms flat against the stone wall. I wanted this, surreal or not.

She wrapped her arms around my butt, pulling me to her face. Her eyes closed, she extended her tongue, licking me from the bottom of my lips to the top, barely grazing my clit with each swipe. She continued teasing my clit until it was hard and swollen.

"Please." I moaned, thrusting my hips against her mouth.

She pulled back the hood of my clit with her thumb and forefinger and electricity shot through me. Holding me tightly against her face, she rested the full length of her tongue against my clit. I reveled in the feeling, committing to memory the softness of Jordan's face between my thighs. She breathed in, pulling my clit into her mouth. My body shuddered, nearing orgasm, but knowing it could possibly end, I forced myself to slow down and savor the pleasure. It was obvious she was in no hurry. I twisted my fingers in her hair and forced her mouth harder against me. She kept her teeth locked on my clit, the tip of her tongue pressed hard against the tip. My body no longer existed. I was soaring high, beyond reality and ecstasy. I could hear the water splashing and my moans echoing off the stones. I ached for release. Suddenly she was still. I opened my eyes. She remained in the same position, her mouth on me, but she was staring up at me. She waited. The longer she stared at me, the more my body trembled.

"Don't stop," I begged.

Her eyes brightened, and she carefully eased two fingers into me, her mouth and tongue continuing their onslaught. The moment she found my G-spot, an orgasm erupted within me. She continued, undaunted by my squeezing walls and my quaking body.

I floated in a cloud of pleasure, vaguely aware of her third and fourth fingers joining the previous two. The combined pleasures of her tongue and fingers awakened a new being in me. I was opening up, blooming for her, desiring and inviting her to take me. Even after I'd had multiple orgasms she was relentless, pushing her fingers deeper into me, reaching and caressing areas never before touched. I pushed against her hand, longing for her completely. Acknowledging my request, she tucked her thumb into her palm and gently pushed. I gasped as her entire hand penetrated me easily. Once in, she held it motionless, allowing my body to accept her on my terms. She leaned back on her knees, her puffy red lips and chin glistening with my wetness.

"Easy," she whispered, "relax, let it happen naturally."

I worked my hips in a slow circular motion while she moved her fist slowly. My sex contracted, released and opened until she was in beyond her wrist. I closed my eyes, overwhelmed by her ability to take me somewhere I'd never been, had never even known existed. She rotated her hand inside me. With smooth even strokes she pulled her hand back a few inches, increasing the intensity and speed as my body responded, my cries echoing off the cave walls.

"I want you," she whispered. The veins on her wrist appeared, only to disappear quickly as she pushed back into me. Again and again, fast and hard. The sight of it pulled me to new levels, swirling silver plains of desire.

"Let yourself go."

Where else could I possibly go? Multiple orgasms, fisting, a woman, could there be more?

"Come on," she coaxed, "share with me."

My body responded, jerking furiously, exploding and releasing. I couldn't comprehend what was happening. My mind whirled, and I floated away.

What seemed like ages later I struggled to open my eyes, my body like wet sand. "What the hell was that?"

She smiled. "You've never experienced anything like that, have you?"

"I thought I was dreaming."

She laughed, a beautiful, deep throaty sound that made me start to throb again. "You might be a bit sore later. But it should take your mind off your ankle."

I returned her grin and stretched like a cat. This was turning into the best camping trip ever.

"Would you like to see the beauty from the top?" she asked.

"The actual waterfall?"

"Sure, my camp is up there and we'll take the trail, which shouldn't be too rough on your ankle...that is, if you'd like to hang around another day? If not, I can take you down to the main trailhead. But if you'd like to stay another day, I can take you back the day after."

Spend another day alone with her? After the past few hours I would practically kill a house full of kittens for five more minutes. I kissed her quickly and felt myself blushing. She deepened it before moving away and helping me stand. We swam back to shore and got dressed in our rumpled, dirty clothes. They felt particularly strange after the amazing way she'd made my body feel.

The hike to the top took several hours. It was hot and my clothes were sticking to me, but her guided tour was worth my irritability. She was a wonderful guide, pointing out wildflowers and blue jays while steering me clear of poison ivy. Every time my ankle began to ache she was there, her arm out for me to lean on.

We got to a point where the trail ended at the river's edge. "We need to swim from here. That will help with the swelling." She glanced down at my ankle, but when her gaze shifted to my shorts, I knew there was no chance of *that* swelling going down. I followed her lead. She held our backpacks over her head, and once again I was struck by how strong she was. I could see her campsite on the opposite side of the stream.

"This is as close as we get to the edge," she said, helping me onto the rock. "The current's too strong and we don't want to go over."

I stood beside her in silence, awed by the swirling water churning madly before it plunged over the edge. But really, her beauty was equal to the waterfall. I stared at her chest as it rose and fell, not realizing her eyes were only half-closed until it was too late. She gave me a wicked grin.

"Sorry," I mumbled, looking away.

"It's okay." She took my hand and placed it over her heart, which pounded against my palm. She put her hand over my heart.

I gasped and my body swayed. It was like there was a current running between us, like the power of the waterfall ran through our arms and into one another's chests.

"Slow down," she whispered, her breath hot on my cheek, "and allow yourself to experience it."

Obeying her, I concentrated. The fresh air was intoxicating. The rushing water soothing. I was floating into the endless blue sky. My heart was racing…no, it was hers. Ours. She was with me. I could feel her as we soared.

She lowered my body onto the rock. The hot sun had warmed it for hours, and it combined with my water-chilled skin perfectly. I heard myself moan as our bodies pressed together. She lifted herself just enough to allow our pelvic bones to touch. My body responded and I thrust my hips up to meet her. I'd never been so ravenous for another person's touch as I was at that moment. We stayed on the rock until the sun was on the way down.

"Plan on keeping that bag to yourself tonight?" she asked.

"Not at all." I spread the sleeping bag on the ground, excited by the prospect of being close to her again.

She lay beside me, her arm resting on her forehead, staring at the sky. "You certainly can't see this in the city."

"It's really not necessary for you to go with me tomorrow."

"Can't risk the chance you might get lost again." She scratched her cheek and sighed dramatically. "Who would come to your rescue?"

I couldn't argue with such a valid point. We built a fire and relaxed in silence for a while. She was staring at the stars when she started to talk.

"I was in love once, many years ago."

I listened intently, sitting by the blazing fire, her hot skin pressed against mine. Something about the woman, the flames dancing in her eyes, the scent of pine floating on the cool night breeze—it all seemed so right.

She tossed more sticks onto the flames.

"Only once?" I asked.

She nodded, concentrating on the fire. "It was stormy. I haven't spoken to her in seven years. But I still think of her often."

"Why didn't it work?"

"Confusion mostly. We loved each other but couldn't commit."

Even across the flames I could feel her pain. Seven years and it was still so raw. No relationship had ever affected me that way.

"We were supposed to meet here," she continued. "We agreed after seven years we would have grown enough to be together again, and we'd meet here. That's why I needed to be at the waterfall. But she didn't come."

Chills raced up my spine. She was waiting on the love of her life and I was there instead. What did that mean? Anything? I wanted to hold her and take away her pain, but it wasn't for me to do. We had some crazy connection, something that had probably changed me in ways I didn't even understand yet, but that was nothing compared to a love she'd waited seven years for.

She stood up and extended her arms. "These woods are my lover now."

I shivered at the finality in her tone. Like she'd given up on love and decided to become a part of nature instead. What was it like to be at one with nature? Magnificent. A twinge of envy pierced me. "I've had many lovers but never a woman or the woods."

Her laughter echoed through the trees and the tension of the conversation faded. "Sounds like we've both had a run of bad luck." She smiled down at me, and the trace of sadness only added to her beauty. "Maybe that's about to change."

The next morning dawned bright and clear. The sound of the waterfall and the chirping of the birds felt like part of me. I stretched and realized sleeping on the ground wasn't nearly such a pain when you were being made love to all night. I sat up and saw that she was already dressed. She sat on the cooler, her chin resting on her fists, staring at me. I smiled, suddenly shy in the light of day.

"We should head out soon, if we're going to get you to the trailhead by noon. I've radioed for someone to pick you up and take you to the lodge, where you can arrange for your trip home. You should still get your ankle looked at too."

A wave of disappointment flooded me. Just like that, it was over. I would go back to the city, she would go back to…whatever she did. I nodded and pulled my things together. When I was ready I faced her, still sitting in that same position, watching me. I shrugged, at a loss for words. She stood with a sigh and led the way, away from the river and down a steep path. It took concentration not to put a foot wrong, which was good, because I couldn't think of a thing to say.

We reached the trailhead and saw other people in the distance. Brad's car was still in the parking lot below, so clearly he hadn't gone chasing after me. Somehow it made me feel better to know I'd had the time of my life without them even knowing.

Jordan cleared her throat and turned to me. "I waited seven years for a woman who didn't show up. In the last forty-eight hours, I decided to stop waiting and move forward." She kissed the backs of my hands and kept her eyes on mine. "Can I see you again?"

I crushed her in an ecstatic hug. "Yes! I'll camp, I'll hike, I'll do whatever. I want to see where this goes."

A bus pulled up and she waved to the driver. "I wrote my details down and put them in your backpack. Call me when you're ready. And if you change your mind, at least let me know you made it home safe."

I kissed her deeply, wanting her to feel what I felt, what we felt on the mountaintop. "Hurry home. I'll be waiting."

LOVE DANCE

Merina Canyon

Emmy had stayed up all night again. She sprawled on the blue-green shag carpet, her chin resting on the windowsill. She waited for the first glimpse of the sun—her signal to crawl into bed exhausted, pull a pillow over her head and sleep facedown until noon or one, or two.

She had been doing this most of a month, ever since Molly left her—for someone else, a *he,* a he that Emmy hated because he sold drugs and had lured her secret girlfriend away.

Now Emmy was in a prison of loneliness and afraid of the dark. Afraid to turn the light out and sleep during the night. She was already eighteen and she had nothing to look forward to, living with her parents and no job, no life.

She had loved Molly with all her heart, and now Molly was gone. Gone with the drug dealer. Gone.

Blaze wanted to change her name from Barbara because she felt that it suited her better. She was a tomboy, raised on the farm with brothers, and all of them did the same chores. She'd just graduated from high school with above-average grades and was going to community college in the fall.

Blaze had a little money she'd saved up from odd jobs, working for the neighbors mostly, mucking out stables and picking apples, berries and peas. She'd gotten quite a bit of money de-tassling corn last summer and now she thought she'd look for something short term in town, maybe make a little more per hour, which she'd need for tuition.

So when she stopped in at the employment office, she was pleased to find that a company downtown called Rayzon was hiring line workers for the summer only. She wasn't sure what Rayzon manufactured, but that didn't bother her, as long as she didn't have to dress up. She drove her old truck (hand-me-down) over to Rayzon and confidently walked into the office.

Emmy's mother yelled at her that morning. "Get your lazy butt out of bed and go apply for this job!"

Emmy sat up scared and then plopped back down. *You gotta be kidding me.*

"I mean it," her mother went on. "You're sleeping your life away. Rayzon is hiring, so get dressed and walk down there!"

Emmy opened her eyes. Her mother was standing over her like the Wicked Witch of the West. "What time is it?"

Her mother did not answer but smacked the newspaper on the bed and went out. She had her own job to get to.

Emmy groaned as she looked at the clock. She'd been asleep two hours.

Blaze asked the secretary for an application, said, "Thank you, ma'am," and sat at a heavy old table, maybe from a library or school, and pulled out her own ballpoint pen, fine-line. She had neat handwriting of which she was proud. It came naturally to her, a talent she shared with her brother, Mike. She could draw, too. Look at something and sketch it on paper. Realistic. Like birds and barns and cows in the pasture. And of course, horses. She still didn't know what Rayzon did, but maybe these skills of hers would come in handy. She was strong, too. Almost as strong as Mike, but he was taller and a year older, so it was to be expected that he could lift more than she could. Her mother told her someday she'd be glad to be a girl. She doubted it.

Blaze was about to start listing her job experience when the office door opened and three people came in, apparently not together, but all arriving at the same time. They all lined up in front of the secretary's desk—*Mrs. McCall* according to the nameplate—and she handed out applications without much chit-chat. There was a tall wiry man with two or three days' stubble who looked angry, a pregnant woman with large, worried eyes and a girl about the same age as Blaze. She looked familiar, cute, sleepy, lost in her own world, a chip on her shoulder, maybe.

Emmy was last in line behind the pregnant woman. She had let the pregnant woman go ahead of her, and that creepy guy should have let her go ahead, too. But he had pushed ahead of the two females and rushed up to the secretary, a middle-aged blonde with a good-natured face. Emmy felt comforted by Mrs. McCall's calmness as she handed out one-page, two-sided applications and invited them to have a seat. Emmy noticed the farm girl over at the table right away. Cowboy boots and faded Levi's. Cute with brown, sun-streaked short hair. She looked familiar. Had they gone to the same school? Emmy hadn't graduated— refused to return after a suspension for smoking, and she hated school anyway after Molly had dropped out. Now she was stuck looking for a stupid, meaningless job. All she wanted to do was write poems and play guitar. She was sure she wouldn't be doing that here at the junk mail factory—if they even wanted her.

The door opened again and Blaze looked up when she heard tiny bells jingling, the kind some girls wore around their ankles. She smiled at the robust hippie woman coming in. The bells weren't on her ankles but were maybe attached to her full skirt or something. Blaze couldn't see where. The woman smelled like an exotic flower, nothing that grew around there. She had long, wavy rusty-red hair flowing around her shoulders, and she seemed to be smiling at nothing in particular. She looked at Blaze and said good morning.

Blaze suddenly felt overly helpful. "You can get an application over there," she said, and nodded toward Mrs. McCall. "And then sit over here and fill it out."

"I'm Dancing Bear," the woman said to the secretary.

"That your real name, hon?" The secretary put on her half glasses. "We need real names here on the application."

"I'll write it down," Dancing Bear said, smiling. "But call me *Dance*. Everyone does."

"Alrighty, Miz Dance. You can fill this out over at that table. Then bring it back."

Blaze was done with her application but she hadn't realized she should take it back to the desk. *You're not in school anymore, dipstick,* she reminded herself and shook her head at her own naïveté.

When she stood up, she caught the sleepy girl staring at her. "Do I know you?" Blaze whispered like she was in a library and could get in trouble.

The sleepy girl said something strange. "Not in the biblical sense." And her pale face remained cold stone serious. "You want to know me, Cowgirl?"

The hippie woman snorted a muffled laugh and jingled as she shifted in her seat.

Blaze saw that the sleepy girl hadn't written a thing. "Ain't you gonna fill that out?"

"'Ain't' ain't a word," the girl said.

"Is that so?" Blaze said, embarrassed but intrigued. She turned away and handed her paper to the secretary, who looked over her half glasses at her pleasantly and said she should wait for the manager to come have a look at it. Blaze spotted a piece of typing paper discarded in the trash basket and delicately retrieved it.

The wiry man was up ready to hand in his application, too. Emmy couldn't stand his energy—all grabby and ugly—a lot like that drug-dealing bastard she hated. Emmy wrote a few lines on her application—basic stuff—and wondered who that cowgirl was. She'd seen her around school for sure but from some other crowd, the farm kids—not her own lot of freaks and misfits. Not that she had friends anymore. Falling in love with your own sex was secret and awkward and isolating. Why did Molly have to leave her? They were so crazy about each other. But Molly said she really wasn't like Emmy—not in that way. The way that Emmy realized she was by age eleven when she fantasized about the teenaged babysitter.

"Can I draw you?"

Emmy looked up to see the cowgirl looking at her, that pen in her hand and a bent piece of typing paper in front of her. "What?"

"Draw you," the cowgirl repeated. "On paper."

"Why?" Emmy said, scrunching up her face.

"'Cuz I can draw. And I draw fast."

"Well, have at it if it turns you on," Emmy said and tried

to look annoyed and disinterested, but in reality she was fascinated.

The cowgirl drew Emmy's hair first—long and straight and parted in the middle. Then she put in delicate eyebrows, looking at Emmy and back down at the paper over and over. Emmy got a tingling sensation from head to toe. This good-looking rodeo girl was touching her all over with her eyes and it felt strangely good—and sexy.

Dance had leaned over and was watching the portrait emerge. "That's cool, sister," she said. "You're quick on the draw."

The cowgirl kept going without comment. Emmy's lips. The delicate crevasse between her nose and lips. Emmy's nose. Her chin. Long, smooth neck. But no eyes. Not yet.

That's when the door opened behind the secretary's desk and a tall principal-looking man stepped into the office. The manager.

Blaze stopped drawing and turned around in her seat. Meanwhile Dance was picking up her application and the sleepy girl's, too, and passing them over to the secretary like they'd just taken a test. Blaze figured this was the manager, and he would either hire her or not. If not, fine. There were other jobs in the world. But something made her really want this one. She was already attached to Dance and the sleepy girl, and she didn't want it to end yet. She sat up straight and ran her fingers through her hair. The man thumbed through the papers, leaning down and pointing out things to the secretary from time to time.

"Aren't you going to finish that work of art?"

Blaze swung back around to answer Dance. "Yeah, I will for sure—right after I get this job."

"You're going to get it," Dance said. "You got the karma. Good things are coming your way, sister."

"You see the future?" Blaze whispered, interested.

"I sense things," Dance said. "It's easy if you can tune in." She closed her long-lashed eyes, and when she opened them she looked right at the sleepy girl.

"Her, too?" Blaze asked. "I mean, getting hired?"

Dance continued to stare at Sleepy Girl, who perked up noticeably. It was like her battery had run down and just by someone looking at her she got charged and the color came into her face.

"Yeah," the girl said. "What's my future?" She fluffed out her straight hair.

Dance looked at Blaze and back at the girl. "You'll see. Good things are coming."

"Okay, folks," the manager man boomed. "Thank you all for coming. I'm Mr. Rex. I'll be taking you through the premises for a look-see, and you'll all start in the morning."

The wiry man let out a whoop and Blaze cracked a smile at him. Poor guy needed a break. *Well, don't we all.* This was something she wanted, too. Whatever it was they made here, she'd do her very best.

Emmy really wanted to see that portrait complete. It was spooky to leave it with no eyes, like she had no windows looking into her soul. But the rest of it looked so real, the eyebrows and everything. She was still tingling from Blaze studying her face, and then Dance looked right into her soul or something. She hadn't wanted to go to work, especially in an uncool place like this, but already she wanted to belong with these two, one fresh off the farm and the other fresh off a hippie commune or whatever. She was glad they weren't going right to work—she was dead tired and hungry—but she could get through an orientation, especially standing close to Blaze.

She stood up with the others and followed behind the cowgirl. Blaze had strong tan hands that looked like they were ready to reach for something to do. Emmy could think of a few things for those hands to do.

"What about the sketch?" Emmy asked.

Dance picked it up. "I'll keep it in my bag for you," she told Blaze, and Blaze did not object. Blaze looked like she was standing at attention waiting for orders from Rex. Emmy couldn't take her eyes off the back pockets of her tight jeans.

"What's your name?" Blaze asked quietly. They were standing in the entry way of a factory room, waiting for Mr. Rex to come open the double doors and tour them around.

"Emmy, but it's really Emma, which I hate."

"Okay. I like Emmy. Nice name." Blaze felt herself redden in the face. She liked this girl a lot, and right at that moment, she lost all her confidence and felt awkward and nervous. Dance was swaying from left to right as though she had her own private music going. The tall guy was silent but jittery, anxious.

Just then Mr. Rex came back and swung open the doors to the factory. "And here we are," he said. "Welcome to Rayzon."

Blaze couldn't believe her eyes. Row after row of people—mostly middle-aged like her parents—sitting at conveyor belts. The sound of the room was like a construction site with motors running and gears and whistles and noise rising up to the high ceiling trying to push its way out. Blaze unconsciously covered her ears, then slid her hands in her back pockets.

A tall, skinny teenaged boy came by pushing a cart full of packages and Blaze thought he gave Emmy the once-over. She suddenly felt an urge to punch him. Was this all a big mistake or was she meant to be here?

* * *

Emmy forced herself to get in bed at midnight with a light still on and the radio playing. She had to sleep if she was going to go through with this job thing, and if it weren't for Blaze, she wasn't sure she could do it. But something about Blaze gave her a new energy, different from what she felt with Molly, but maybe just as good. *Better?* She would sleep with the light on and the radio would keep her company, but she did not have much control over her thoughts of Molly. She cried a little remembering how Molly had loved her—however briefly—how damn good love felt, and sex! Even if you did have to keep it a secret because a lot of people would say you were a pervert. And then her thoughts drifted to Blaze and how good she looked in jeans and boots and how innocent she was in a way and strong, and the drawing...Emmy wanted to see that drawing finished! Would Blaze remember?

When Emmy's mother woke her the next morning, she was surprised that she had been in a deep sleep. She woke with a start, filled with anticipation, climbed out of bed without moaning and groaning, and got in the shower.

Blaze sat in the old truck waiting for it to be closer to 8 A.M. She was always early. It was easy for her—up at first light, right to work with chores, everything lined up and ready to go. But this morning wasn't so easy. She was tired. A rare thing for her. She could barely sleep. She'd tossed and turned all night with thoughts of the sleepy girl—Emmy—and she wasn't sure what to say or do about it. There was just something about that girl she liked—really liked—and she couldn't wait to see her again. At the same time it scared her to death! Get involved with another girl? Know her in the *biblical* sense? It wasn't the kind of thing you could go home and tell your family about, and Blaze wasn't used to keeping secrets.

"Howdy, partner."

It was Dance, now standing outside Blaze's open truck window. She was all dressed in purple and pink with a beaded headband across her forehead holding her thick goddess hair in place.

"Morning, Dancing Bear," Blaze said. She wondered where Dance had come from. It was like she just suddenly materialized. "Are you ready for this?"

"It's just a stepping stone in life," Dance said, smiling. "I can do it for a while. Then it's time to move on."

"Yeah, me too, I guess." Blaze recalled how overwhelming the graying robotic people sitting at conveyor belts stuffing bubble envelopes with free samples seemed. How long had some of them been there in that dark, dusty cave? It felt too cooped up for Blaze. She'd much rather be out driving a tractor or planting trees.

"It's going to be okay, sister," Dance said. "You'll find love in the strangest places, and it's up to you what you do with it."

Blaze thought that was a really strange thing to say, but she liked the way Dance talked, like she saw something other people didn't and she was here to tell you something.

Emmy was afraid she was late after she'd jogged down the hill to Rayzon and she was deeply relieved to see both Blaze in that cool, old pickup and cosmic Dancing Bear swaying in the parking lot. Dance waved her over and Blaze climbed out of the truck and shut the door hard. She was wearing a black long-sleeved shirt—faded—with pearl snaps. Her boots looked worked-in, scuffy but recently polished.

All three turned their heads when an old VW Bug pulled up with the wiry guy in the passenger seat. He leaned over and kissed the woman driving and got out with a big grin on his face.

The woman handed him a paper bag through the car window.

"We better go in," Dance said, acting like a mother hen. Emmy wondered how old she was. Not old but not young either.

Inside, the secretary nodded at them and called the manager to take them to their jobs. Meanwhile more people were lining up to fill out applications. Emmy recognized the worried-eyed pregnant woman turning hers in.

The manager took Blaze, Dance, Emmy and the wiry man into the noisy workroom and sat them at a conveyor belt that had been completely empty except for a gray-haired woman standing at one end waiting for them.

Emmy was delighted that Blaze would be sitting on her right and Dance on her left.

"Folks, this is Madge," the manager said. "She'll get you started here. Do like she says and have a nice day." He acted like a robot, delivering his lines and rushing off.

Madge didn't crack a smile or anything. In a thick German accent, she told the wiry man to stand at the opposite end of the belt from her. When she put the bubble envelopes on the belt, they were to each insert a trial-size cosmetic. Then wiry man was to collect all the envelopes, run them through a sealer machine and stack them in a cart.

I can do this in my sleep, Emmy thought as she glanced over at Blaze's strong hands ready to get started. She was ready to get started, too, in more ways than one. But could Blaze like her the way she liked Blaze, or was she going to turn out like Molly? The thought of Molly gave her a sinking feeling as the envelope arrived in front of her and she inserted a cherry-flavored lip balm.

Dancing Bear had seen this before: two young women undeniably attracted to each other, their skin tingling with possibility, the thoughts and fantasies crowding up their heads. Yes, she had seen this before, the hesitation, the concern for what was considered normal, the flirtation, again the hesitation, and she had helped, and she would help again. Sometimes she felt that she was plopped down into situations like this to be the silent mediator, bringing together two energies that needed each other. These two had auras merging all over the place and the colors were hot, urgent. This should be good. A miracle, all this earthly attraction and delight.

Dancing Bear pulled little shampoo bottles from a box with her left hand and popped them into the envelopes with her right hand. She could feel the heat in Emmy's heart, a heart recently broken but now laying itself open for more. Blaze had already set a fire going in that heart, and Dancing Bear would fan the flames. She had the almost-done portrait still in her bag and she'd encourage Blaze to take it home and finish it. The result would rock Emmy's world. Dance could already see it. The two of them were lovers already on a plane they could not see, and already they were completely in tune with the attraction of nature.

Blaze was nervous as she sat behind her steering wheel with Emmy in her passenger seat. They had known each other a total of seven days, but not in the biblical sense, of course. Not yet. Maybe not ever, but Blaze hoped Emmy liked her as much as she liked Emmy because Blaze felt like she was just about to bust wide open, and if it wasn't mutual...well, then...but it sure looked mutual and Dance had told her to follow her *bliss,* whatever that meant, and that it was okay to love anybody you wanted to.

"Are you going to give it to me or what?" Emmy snapped with an edge of lust and laughter in her voice.

"Just hold your horses, little lady," Blaze shot back. "I got it right here in this folder." She reached behind her seat for the folder that held the finished portrait.

"Finally," Emmy said.

Blaze had taken time to shade it in, add color and get those eyes that she had come to adore just right. She opened the folder, proud of her work.

Emmy scooted over to Blaze on the front seat and stared into her own face. She instantly teared up, which she wasn't expecting. The girl in the portrait looked so poetically pained. The eyes— hurt, smart, surprised at the depth of brokenheartedness. The long windblown hair, the smooth chin, all of it spoke of something Emmy could not name right now. She felt Blaze's arm around her shoulder. She felt her own head sink into Blaze's chest. She felt Blaze kiss the top of her head. Emmy wanted to hold this position as long as possible, hoping no one could see them in the deserted lot after work. She listened to Blaze's pumping heart and smiled. She felt her own heart, too, and the rising of a powerful desire. Dance had told Emmy that love was in reach and that she shouldn't be afraid to reach out again. She lifted her face and met Blaze's lips. The kiss was delicate and desperate. Emmy wanted to say I love you already, but she knew better than that. Wait. The perfect moment would come.

"Oh god," Blaze said. "What you've done to me!"

"I'm going to keep doing it," Emmy said, touching places all over Blaze's beautiful strong body. "Right here and here and here and here."

LIKE A BREATH OF OCEAN BLUE

Elizabeth Black

There was something magical about the ocean in the height of summer. Warm air crackled around me, as if the sky knew this day was going to be special. I stood by the store's back door, drinking a cup of coffee and watching the gulls bob up and down on the ocean's waves.

I minded the T-shirt store Monday through Friday from nine to five. Today, being Friday, was a special day. My heart thundered in my chest. *She'll arrive any minute.* This was the first time I had interest in a woman more than merely daydreaming about her. I fingered the necklace in my pocket. *Am I being too forward giving it to her? What if she doesn't like women?* I'd longed for a woman's touch for many years but never found an opportunity until I met Malena.

Malena—her name was an elixir on my lips. Ma-le-na. An orgasm in my mouth. Like a breath of ocean blue, she caught me in the pull of her riptide. Malena, whose hair fell down her back like dark rain during a midnight storm. Her sun-kissed skin glowed the color of the coffee and cream I sipped every morning.

I admired her body from afar: a swell of broad hips that kissed her waist the way I wanted to, shoulders broad enough for me to rest my head upon, breasts so full I could get lost in all that delicious cleavage.

How I longed for Malena, but I was too chicken-hearted to make a move.

She was a virago on the waves of the churning ocean. Try as I might, I couldn't keep up with her. No one could. After all, how do you hold the wind in your hands? She slipped through—teasing, tormenting—and a lighthearted laugh burst from her supple lips each time she saw the agony she put me in.

She made a deal with the owner of the shop to live upstairs while she tended to the store on weekends and the summer holidays no one else wanted to work. She slept to the sound of waves crashing on the beach. I envied her. I wished I lived in a home that backed up to the ocean. I didn't know what other deals she made to have gained such wonderful sleeping arrangements. All I knew was that I wanted her to myself.

Each weekend when she stormed into my life, I swore I would make a move on her. I flirted and blushed at her every word. I often had her favorite coffee waiting for her when she came in—black coffee with Kahlúa. Sometimes I plied her with a cherry cheese danish. She loved cherries. Each time she smiled at me with gratitude I melted inside. She seemed to enjoy my attention, but could I be sure she wouldn't balk if I took a step further? I feared she'd recoil from me in disgust.

But what if she didn't?

She kept me company in the store on Fridays and Mondays, and she occasionally even helped me fold T-shirts the tourists had tossed into a heap on the floor. The longer we kept each other company, the more I wanted her.

This day, I was determined to make her my own, if only I would stop chickening out! I wore my most flattering miniskirt and my favorite white cotton blouse. I dabbed ocean-scented oil along my throat, behind my ears, between my breasts, and I smoothed it through my hair. I had to look and smell my best for when I gave Malena her big surprise. My July Fourth gift to her burned a hole in my pocket. I would give it to her when the moment was right. It was an offering to a goddess in the hope she would approve and cast upon me the affection I so desperately wanted.

When she burst through the front door it was like a zephyr had entered, disrupting even the air around her. At the sound of her laugh, my body tingled as if her honeyed voice dripped down my skin. I wanted to lick her off, slowly.

"Katie, my Kate! Help! I'm going to drop everything!" She approached me, arms burdened with grocery store bags. I grabbed a few in one hand, carrying my coffee in the other, and followed her up the stairs. The scent of seaweed and ocean air surrounded her as if she burst from the sea itself. Her bum swayed as she climbed the stairs. It took all my willpower to keep from reaching out and squeezing one ample cheek.

The upstairs was a study in shades of cream and sea foam that offset Malena's tan. We raced to the open kitchen and dropped bags on the marble counter. She tossed food into the refrigerator pell-mell, which was her style. Malena was not a neat woman. Her life, like her spirit, was chaos. Without wasting a moment, she rummaged through the last bag until she found a bottle of Kahlúa and a quart of heavy cream. This wasn't heavy cream from the grocery store. It was thick and mouth-watering heavy cream from a local dairy. Malena did not skimp on the second deadly sin.

"A treat for us!" Her smile brightened the already white-bright room. "Kahlúa for your coffee and a Kahlúa and cream on ice for me."

"Isn't it a little early for alcohol?"

She touched my cheek, leaving a flame of desire on my skin in her wake. "Of course it is. That's why I pour it in your coffee. The perfect breakfast pick-me-up." Without waiting for an invitation, she grabbed my coffee, removed the plastic lid and poured in a healthy stream of Kahlúa.

I could make a move on her now if I wished. Embrace her after she handed me my coffee. *No, I can't do this. It's better she never knows how I feel about her.*

"I can't stay. I have to get back downstairs."

"Nonsense. The shop doesn't open up for another hour. How long does it take you to set up? Ten, fifteen minutes? No rush. You've locked the front door, right?"

"Yes."

"Then stop worrying about it. Drink."

She handed my cup to me, and I sipped. The smoothness of Kahlúa mellowed the bitterness of my coffee. Malena was right—a little alcohol in the morning was a lovely pick-me-up. It also calmed me down. Why not enjoy basking in her presence for an hour even if I didn't so much as brush my hand against her cheek?

"How does it taste? Better?" she asked.

"Much."

Without warning, she ran her finger along the corner of my mouth. I shivered at her unexpected touch. My heart soared. Was she flirting with me? I hoped so!

"Some coffee got away from you. Can't have you dribbling down your chin." She smiled. "At least, not about coffee." Before I could ask what she meant, she continued. "I'm glad I caught you before the shop opened for the day. Do you have plans for this weekend?"

What could she possibly want with me? The fact that she

had shown interest in my schedule enticed me. Did she want to spend time with me? My dream come true!

"No, I don't have any plans. I was going to go to the bonfire on the beach for July Fourth but nothing special. Why?" I was so anxious for her answer my heart nearly ceased to beat.

"I'm having a party, and I want to invite you."

Once again, she touched my cheek, but this time her touch lingered like the caress I wished it were. "I've seen you here every Friday and Monday for the past two months and we've danced around each other. Why is that?"

She cocked her head and smiled at me, making me feel warm and gooey inside. Before I could answer, she raced past me heading for the French doors leading to the balcony overlooking the ocean. When she threw open the doors, the sound of waves crashing on the rocks below soared into the room, making my head spin with delight. Sun shone through Malena's linen miniskirt. She wore no underwear. Her ass teased me, shaped like a firm peach. My gaze traveled from her well-formed, cinnamon-toned calves up the back of her legs until I eyed the shadow of where those legs met. I wanted her. The scent of the ocean lingered around Malena and floated toward me. Here was my chance.

"Ah, that's better. I love the sound and smell of the surf when I stay here," she said. "I even keep the doors open during thunderstorms. There's something exciting about the crackle of static electricity in the air, isn't there?"

There doesn't need to be a thunderstorm for this room to crackle with static electricity as long as you're standing in it. "I love storms, and I'd love to come to your party. Is it here?" I croaked, voice hoarse with excitement.

"Yes. It's tomorrow night after I close shop."

I walked toward her, not wanting her to be so far away from

me for even an instant. We moved to the deck. Hot sun beat down upon my shoulders, but it couldn't rival the heat coming from Malena's body. She made me feel alive. Without needing an invitation, she placed one hand on my shoulder. My entire body tingled at her touch. In such close proximity, she felt free to stare at me, her emerald gaze seeking out my soul. Her smile warmed the air around us.

"I've been watching you, Katie, my Kate, and I want to ask you something."

"What?"

"Would you like to spend the evening with me, just the two of us, alone?"

My body shook with anticipation of the meaning of her innocent words. Maybe she only wanted my company. A girl's night together, drinking Kahlúa and cream, listening to the splashing surf and basking in the summertime glow of the sun beating down upon the beach.

I hoped she wanted more.

"Yes, I would love to spend the evening with you." I swallowed hard and asked a leading question I hoped would spur her interest. "Do you have something special in mind?"

"I do. And I think you'd enjoy it. After all, I've seen the way you've watched me since we first laid eyes on each other. When I catch you unawares, you blush—just as you are now!"

She ran a finger down my cheek, bringing prickly heat to the surface. I probably glowed as red as a burn by now.

"Your shyness is so sweet. I love it," she said. "I've taken notice of your lovely gifts of coffee and danish, and I know they're more than courtesies of a work colleague. I may not have said a word, but I'm not naïve."

When she spoke, her voice was so soft I barely heard her, but her words revealed my deepest, most intimate fantasies. Her fingers weaved through my hair, pulling my head toward hers. Her eyes, aflame, gazed into mine, and I felt as if she touched my very soul.

"I know you've wanted to do this for a very long time. So have I. The difference between us is I take what I want."

Her lips brushed mine, cool in the warm summer heat. I closed my eyes and lost myself in her kiss. The scent of ocean surf mingled with her crisp perfume. Lips parted, and tongues danced a salsa around each other. I had never before kissed a woman. Her lips were feather soft, like pillows pressing against my lips. So unlike a man's. Her delicate cheek brushed against my chin, so smooth. For once a face brushed my own that was not covered with stubble.

This was where I belonged, in Malena's arms, wrapped in her sumptuous curves.

"You don't have to be downstairs for another fifty minutes," she whispered against my throat. The warm breath on my skin made me break out in goose bumps. "I can help you pass the time. It will fly by quickly."

"Too quickly," I said as I stroked her back. She felt smaller than she looked; a tiny thing ready to burst out of her own skin. At long last, I felt the weight of Malena's supple body in my arms. Her full breasts pressed against my chest. Her arms wrapped around me like trembling vines around a solid oak. Despite her casual attitude, she was as nervous about our tryst as I was. How many times had she miscalculated the interest of a woman she desired? At least this time, her hunch was correct.

The sound of the churning waves kept time with the urgent beating of my heart. With fumbling fingers, I unbuttoned my blouse and let it drape across my shoulders, hiding my breasts. What if she didn't like how they were shaped? They were pendulous, inferior compared to her full and high magnificence. I dreaded the possibility she would not like my body and would reject my attention.

Malena stared at my breasts, her expression wide open and full of desire. I relaxed, as I had nothing to fear after all.

"You aren't wearing a bra," she said.

"Bras make me feel uncomfortable in hot, sticky weather." The truth was, I stopped wearing one because I had dreamed of a moment like this.

"Let me show you hot and sticky." She slid the blouse down my arms until she held it in one hand. I stood before her, bare-breasted, waiting for one of us to make a move. Her free hand lingered on my wrist, stroking it in such a way I was sure she could feel my racing pulse.

"You're lovely. Such soft skin..." Her lips brushed against the tender skin above my left breast with a butterfly kiss so delicate she took my breath away.

"Katie, my Kate, you're beautiful. I should have told you that a long time ago." Warm lips pressed my skin and her tongue snaked out, lapping at my flushed chest. My knees shook so much I could barely stand. *Finally*. She stroked me the way I had dreamed for the past two months, and I didn't even need to make a move.

Her hands alighted on my hips, gently kneading the tension out of my muscles. Every one of my nerve endings burned with longing. Her mere touch sent shocks of hot electric lust across the entire surface of my body. When she brushed her lips to my nipple I took in a deep breath and held it for what seemed like eternity. My heart trip-hammered in my throat. I gripped her thick hair in my hands as her tongue worked my nipple until it stood erect. She wrapped her lips around my bud, pulling gently as a thrill of excitement ran from my breasts, down my belly, to slam deep in my pussy. I stroked her back and inhaled the salty ocean scent trapped in her lustrous hair.

When I pulled at the hem of her tank top, she raised her head and gazed with lust and affection into my eyes. Without saying a word, she slipped her tank top over her head and tossed it onto the deck. Her breasts stood tall and firm before me, bronzed and glistening with droplets of sweat. She had no tan lines. The image of Malena sunbathing topless on the deck ignited my lust. I pressed my hands against those massive breasts, squeezing hard until she mewled with delight. I lifted them in my hands, feeling their heaviness. I had often fondled my own breasts, but feeling Malena's made her more real in my eyes.

I pinched her nipples until they were so hard they could cut glass. I sucked on her nipples; the taste of salt and coconut oil on her creamy skin exploded in my mouth. Her skin felt like brushed silk. I smoothed my hands along her breasts and down her tight belly. Her belly rippled as my fingers brushed against her skin, and she giggled in my ear. Ticklish, my dear? I wanted to bring forth the same aroused sensations in Malena that she brought forth in me, but I wasn't sure how. I'd never before made love to a woman.

As if sensing my naïveté, she backed me up, slowly, hands stroking my hips until the backs of my calves felt the hardness of a wooden chaise lounge.

I sat, stretching my legs out in front of me. Malena knelt between them and pushed my legs apart. Her fingers drifted along my inner thighs, drawing figure eights along my skin until she reached beneath my skirt. I lay back upon the chair, arching my spine as her fingers touched the satin of my panties. How I longed for her fingers to reach beneath the fabric and caress my heat. Instead, she caught my panties in her hands and tugged at them. I lifted, and she pulled my panties down my legs until they landed on the deck. Bare-bottomed, I felt exposed but eager before my tanned goddess.

She slipped off my sandals and took my feet into her hands. Using her thumbs, she pressed hard into my arches. My feet curled at her touch, reflecting the way my body curled into itself on the chair. I was a fractal before her, curl upon curl upon devilish curl. Eyes closed, I pinched my nipples until they stood on end. I gave my body and will over to her, coiling with erotic delight as her mouth found my toes. Her warm tongue sucked on one toe at a time, dipping in between each that drove me into an erotic frenzy so intense I wanted to throw her on the deck and take her.

Malena had other plans.

She kissed my ankles and brushed up my calves, leaving a soft trail of moisture in her wake. My blood flowed like the rising and setting tides, heartbeat thundering throughout. Only Malena could pull such exquisite joy from me. Oh, my darling goddess. Her lips against my thighs tickled. I had no idea I was ticklish there. My nerve endings were raw and frayed in Malena's grasp. My skin screamed with delight at her mere touch. As she approached my heat, it took all my willpower not to push her face to me.

The moment her tongue licked my lips, I let out a groan so deep I felt it in my solar plexus rather than heard it. She lapped at me, teasing my lips until they were so full of blood and so overly sensitive I had to pull away. She would have none of that. She gripped my hips and held me fast while she buried her face against me. I didn't want to be without her touch for even a moment. My fingers dug into her scalp, scratching amid her thick hair, pressing her head so hard against me I momentarily feared she couldn't breathe. Her tongue lashed at my sex, lapping my sopping pussy like an eager kitten lapping a bowl of thick, heavenly cream. And what a kitten she was!

Malena knew exactly where to direct the fevered motions of her talented tongue. She flicked my clit ever so gently, as if she knew I'd feel overly sensitive by direct touch. She had the precision of a surgeon, and she knew exactly where to place her glorious tongue to drive me mad.

She massaged my bum and then the small of my back as she lifted my hips to give her greater access to my sex. She flattened her tongue against my lips and slowly licked back and forth along the entire length until I was in such agonizing arousal I begged her to finish me off. She'd have none of that either.

"I'm going to make you come so hard you'll crawl down the stairs on all fours," she whispered. "And you'll come when I say so. Understand?"

"Yes, but don't be so cruel. I can't bear this agony much longer."

Her deep-throated laugh rang in my ears. "Your agony is my pleasure, and I'll make it the best pleasure you've ever felt. Just lie back and enjoy yourself. I'll help you get through the day, and we'll be together alone this evening to continue where we leave off."

Before I could answer, she took my tender clit between her soft lips. I writhed beneath her, oversensitive bud crying out in sheer ecstasy. Malena moaned a laugh. The reverberations vibrated through my pussy, and I tightened around the finger she somehow slipped inside me without my being completely aware of it. I gripped that finger, and then she slid in two, then three, all the while working her magic on my clit. Her tongue flicked in circles around my clit, not directly on it, and I took the break to breathe, but I shouldn't have let my guard down.

She licked one finger and slipped it into my anus, and with a cry I arched my back as a roiling orgasm ravished my body. Over and over I came, like never before, one orgasm subsiding into another to crest and flow again. I gripped her fingers as I rode her hand, bucking so hard against the chaise lounge it jumped on the deck. Warm fluid spurted from deep inside to slick my thighs and bum. Sweat on my forehead and chest beaded on my skin, tickling me as it dripped down fine hair. My pulse pounded in my ears with an orgasm more intense than any I'd ever before felt.

I opened my eyes, and the sun seemed unbearably bright. The salty scent of the surf intensified in the air around me. The blue of the sky grew deeper and the song of gulls crashed in my ears. My senses had gone into overdrive as my body melted in the afterglow of my climax. Malena lifted her head from me, wiped her face clean with the back of her hand and licked the fingers that had been in my pussy, smiling at me in her own bewitching way.

"I won't bathe so I may smell your scent on me all day." She smiled. "I've wanted to ravish you since we first met. I wonder what took so long?"

"I wasn't sure if you were into women. I should have made a move earlier."

She caressed my cheek, and I bent my head into her palm as if offering myself to her.

"I knew you wouldn't. You're too shy. It has always been up to me, but you actually did make the first move by showering me with all that attention. You sent very clear signals. It was up to me to read them properly."

She stood and straightened her skirt, but she did not put on her tank top. Her breasts teased me as they bobbed and swayed, begging for my touch, but I knew I was out of time. Malena took me by the hand, helped me rise and kissed me on the lips. I tasted my essence as her tongue slipped into my mouth.

"At 5:05, I expect to see you up here, ready to continue where we left off."

"And I'll return the favor."

She smiled. "I look forward to it."

I slipped back into my clothes and then felt the gift in my skirt pocket. "Ah, before I forget, speaking of showering you with attention, I have a gift for you. I saw this at one of the shops and it had your name written all over it."

When Malena saw the delicate necklace I pulled from my pocket, her face lit up. She took it from me and held it up to the sunlight.

"It's beautiful! I love it! Since it's from you, I'll cherish it always." She fingered shards of glass, their edges softened by years of riding the tides. Blue matched the ocean water and emerald matched her eyes. Small shells hung between rice pearls holding the necklace together.

"Think of me when you wear it. Let me put it on you," I said.

She turned away from me and lifted her hair. I unclasped the necklace and fastened it around her swanlike neck. Her café-au-lait skin brought out the sheer colors of the jewels and shells.

"You look beautiful. As always," I said.

She swept me up in her arms and kissed me again, full on the lips. Our tongues tangled, never wanting to let go. When she pulled away, I groaned with disappointment.

"I'll never take it off," she said. "I'll have a good meal ready for us when you come upstairs."

"And then back to the deck and the chaise lounge?"

"Or my bed." She grinned.

I wanted to make love under the light of the moon with the crashing waves our only witnesses. As I tidied my dress, Malena picked up my satin panties and held them to her face. She closed her eyes and inhaled deeply, taking in the very essence of my being.

"I'm keeping these. I want to be reminded of you all day. Go commando and think of me."

"I can't stop thinking about you." I drew her into my arms and kissed her, feeling my body melt into hers as if we belonged together. Which we did.

"Until 5:05," I said.

"I'll be waiting for you."

I headed down the stairs to prepare for the day. Fresh coffee and Kahlúa in hand, I sipped as the hours sped by until I could be in Malena's arms again, where I belonged. I didn't want to be anywhere else, knowing the ocean's tides would witness our love again that evening.

WIGGLE-WIGGLE-WOMP

D. Jackson Leigh

The soft slap of my sneakers echoed rhythmically in the silence of the third-floor corridor ringing the coliseum. Except for the occasional straggler looking for the VIP lounge's free beer, the hallway was empty, just the way I felt.

We always came to the basketball tournament together. It was the highlight of our year—four days of beautiful, athletic female bodies, gladiators of the court pushing their abilities and opponents as far as possible. We both loved the competition, the cheering, the greasy hot dogs and roasted pecans. We loved getting to know the people sitting around us, strangers at the beginning and new friends by the time the tournament ended.

Sure, plenty of those tournament friends, as well as our personal friends, filled the generous seating this year. But she had to work over the weekend and her absence licked the red off my candy, spoiled the milk in my cereal, let the air out of my fun. We always came together. I wanted to whine, but settled for silent sulk and another solitary trip around the coliseum's circumference.

I glanced up at the periodic TV monitor near the end of my fifth lap. The next game was about to begin. I sighed. The friends I was sitting with would wonder where I'd gone. First, a pit stop. I pushed through the door to the ladies' restroom. The top-tier seating wouldn't fill up until the last two days of the tournament, so there was no line. Just empty stalls.

I was about to flush when I heard the door open and someone come in. I expected it was one of the bored spouses cajoled into attending the tournament because her partner loved basketball. The VIP lounge was usually filled with them, drinking the tournament away while their more sober partners were downstairs actually watching the action.

When I exited the stall, the newcomer was leaning against the row of sinks, playing with a tiny toy badger. She was really cute—short black spiky hair and blue, blue eyes. I'm a sucker for blue eyes. She pressed the badger's paw and set it on the long vanity. It shook its furry little butt as it inched along the sinks. "Wiggle-wiggle-womp," it growled out in a grumpy old man voice before reciting a plug for a local car dealership.

I smiled at her. "Cute."

She looked up from the toy and cocked her head. "You think so?"

I shrugged. "In a weird kind of way, I guess. Where'd you get it?"

"I saw it on a local TV commercial, so I went to the dealership and bought one."

"Huh. Didn't know they sold them. The commercials are pretty popular, though."

"So, you live here?"

"Not in Greensboro, but only about two hours away." I dried my hands and took aim at the trash receptacle. The wadded paper towel arced perfectly across the room and joined the rest of the trash. "We're all about basketball in North Carolina."

"Three points," she said, acknowledging my score. "Then you can be my first test subject." She held out her hand. "I'm Haley."

I smiled and took her hand in mine. "I'm Logan."

"Pleased to meet you." She held up the toy. "Interested?"

Not in that toy. I dropped my gaze in an obvious sweep of her toned body. "In being your test subject?"

Her face reddened, but she grinned at my response. "Yes. I'm working with the WNBA to put together marketing profiles for two new expansion teams. One of the locations under consideration is Portland, Oregon. So, I'm thinking the Portland Badgers." She squeezed the badger's paw again and we watched its butt wiggle as it chanted its slogan. "I was thinking there must be a way to work that wiggle-wiggle-womp into our marketing material."

"You're kidding, right?"

She raised her eyebrows. "No. I'm totally serious. I can see it now. The Badgers make a really big play and the fans stand up, turn their butts to the opposing team and—" She pressed the badger's paw a third time and turned around to demonstrate. "Wiggle-wiggle-womp. Wiggle-wiggle-womp."

She chanted along with the toy and shook the cutest ass I'd ever seen. After I un-swallowed my tongue, I began to laugh. The more I laughed, the more she performed.

She finally stopped and turned back to me. "See? You love it."

I nodded enthusiastically. "I'm ready to buy season tickets."

She winked at me. "Thanks for the input."

"Are you going downstairs?" I hoped, I hoped. "The next game must have started by now, and I have an empty seat next to mine."

She shook her head. "I've got some business to take care of, but maybe I'll see you around later." She picked up her furry friend. "Enjoy the games this afternoon."

Then she was gone, and I was left with nothing but the throb between my legs. I briefly considered ducking into a stall to take care of that. Two minutes max. Instead, I decided to enjoy the sweet ache as a reminder of her dance and the possibility that I might see her again.

Later that night the throb was in my ears, the pounding in my head.

I usually loved the after-games parties. Drinking and dancing and drinking. It was the one time each year we sprang for an expensive hotel room so we could attend the raucous lesbian gathering downstairs and just stumble upstairs to fall into bed.

My heart, however, wasn't in it tonight. My girl wasn't here. No slow dances. No stolen kisses. No dark corner groping. It sucked the life out of my party.

I stirred my drink and sank deeper into my pout. My friends were getting obnoxiously inebriated. The disco-themed music was too loud, and the alcohol in my drink was making my sinuses swell. I wondered if my friends were drunk enough for me to slip up to my quiet room where I could lie in the dark and mourn my ruined vacation.

"Is this seat taken?"

I turned and fell into those Carolina blue eyes, completely forgetting that I'm a die-hard Duke fan. The night suddenly didn't seem so dark.

I grinned at her. "I was holding it for you."

She waved at a waitress carrying a tray of drinks. "Over here," she said.

The waitress unloaded two tall cranberry and vodkas and

eight shots of buttery nipple, and then disappeared with a smile and a ten-dollar tip.

"I call this 'sweet-tart,'" she said, smiling at me.

I looked over the selection of drinks, and then at her. "Uh, Haley, right?" Damn, she had cute dimples.

"That's right." She divided the drinks between us and held up the first of her four shot glasses. "To the Badgers."

I grabbed a shot glass and downed it with her, then sipped my Cape Cod. She was right. The sweetness of the butterscotch schnapps was a great contrast to the tart cranberry juice. She was sweet to buy the drinks for us, and the alcohol left me feeling like a bit of a tart. I lifted a second shot. "To the bluest eyes in Carolina."

She downed the second with me and grinned as she picked up the third. "To tall, sexy Duke fans."

Oh, yeah. The vacation was saved. The song segued into an old Donna Summer tune and I made a final toast. "To bad girls."

We tossed back the last of our buttery nipples, and I took a big gulp of my Codder before she grabbed my hand and led me to the dance floor. Four songs later the pounding in my ears and sinuses had dropped to my groin. My blood pumped with the music and the sway of her hips. My eyes followed the tiny drop of perspiration that trickled down her temple and along her jawline, and then stopped at her very kissable lips pursed in concentration as she danced. They were moving now. She was talking. But my ears, my thoughts were filled with bad girls, and I only blinked at her.

So she gestured as though she was drinking something and led me back toward our table. We were winding through the crowd behind the waitress with another laden tray when a drunk stumbled into her. I whipped an arm around Haley's waist and tried to yank her out of the way, but the tray of drinks hit her thighs and soaked her pants down past her knees.

"Sorry," the drunk muttered before staggering off.

"I'm so sorry," the waitress said. "Let me get you a towel."

Haley looked down at her dripping pants. "I'm not sure a towel is going to be much help."

"I have a room upstairs," I offered. "I'm sure I have some sweats I can loan you."

"Really? That'd be great," she said.

I took her hand in mine for our walk to the elevators and didn't relinquish it even when others crowded in with us or when I had to dig my room key from my pocket and unlock the door. She turned to me as soon as the door closed. Our eyes met and she touched my cheek. Her lips tasted of cranberries, her tongue of butterscotch. She moaned and I'd swear the national anthem was playing as she fumbled with the buttons on my shirt. Was that the starting buzzer sounding in my head? Play ball.

We struggled with each other's clothing, but I won the toss, coming away with her pants. I passed them off to the chair and walked her backward to the bed to set up the play. She yanked me down on top of her in a woman-on-woman defense, but I blocked her attempt to get a hand down my pants and came away with her panties.

I was ready to make my play.

I drove right down the middle, laying nips and kisses down her neck, pushing her T-shirt up to taste her breasts and belly, and then leapt forward when I found the lane wide open. She was hot and swollen and salty-sweet on my tongue. Her moans filled the room. Her defense was failing. I could have scored easy points. Instead, I eased back to use up more of the clock.

She writhed under me. "Please, I need to come."

The shot clock was running close, so I went for the score. I let my teeth scrape along her turgid clit as I sucked her in.

"Fuck!" Her eyes went wide and her body rigid when I filled her with my fingers to show her my best stroke. Her body bowed and she screamed.

Score. We both panted from the exertion.

She pushed me back and tugged at my pants. I realized that although my shirt was half-unbuttoned and my pants hanging open, I was still dressed. "Off," she said.

She had possession now, and she wasn't ready to call a time out. I love a woman with stamina.

I stood and dropped my pants and underwear to the floor. I was so ready, my stomach clenched. I moved to straddle her shoulders in hopes that she'd take advantage of the open court and go for the fast break, but she had other ideas.

She grabbed the front of my shirt, jerking me to the bed. A clear foul, but I liked physical play. She rolled me onto my back and ripped my shirt off, buttons flying across the room. Okay. That was definitely a charging violation, but her mouth covered mine and swallowed my protest.

Fast break was definitely not in her plans. She took her time, exploring my mouth with her tongue and my body with her hands. I shivered when she licked my pulse and dragged her nails low across my belly. I shuddered when her teeth clamped down hard and her tongue flicked against my taut nipple. And I whimpered when her fingers began to stroke where I needed her most.

God, I needed to come. I bucked my hips to encourage her to stroke harder, faster, but she bit down on my shoulder and flung her leg across my thighs to pin me to the bed. She was setting this tempo now.

Then she stopped. "Time out," she said, releasing me and jumping to her feet.

"Wha-what? Where are you going?" I was rattled. Did I drop the ball? Miss a call?

She grabbed her pants and ran into the bathroom. "I don't want these stains to set. These are my favorite pants."

I could hear water running. Seriously? I'm lying here with my clit hanging out and so near the edge. I slide my hand down my belly and into my soaked curls.

"*Don't touch yourself.*"

I jumped when she yelled. How did she know? She couldn't possibly see through the bathroom wall. I rolled onto my side, but she slipped in behind me before I could box her out. I was bigger and stronger, but she had momentum on her side and rolled me onto my stomach, her weight pinning me. Before I could regroup, her thumb was inside me and her fingers slid over my clit.

"Oh, fuck." Her hand was ice cold against my overheated sex and the contrast was strangely arousing. She stroked me inside and out, inside and out until I buried my face in the pillow and yelled my surrender.

Game over. She'd definitely bested me.

She pulled out slowly as she peppered consolation kisses across my shoulders. She smoothed her hand down the arch of my back and over my bare ass. "I can see a lot of potential here," she said, stroking my glutes.

"What? Wasn't that enough of a spanking you just gave me?"

"Mmm. The score was close, but I think I won." She climbed off the bed and I flopped onto my back to watch in fascination. She still wore her T-shirt, but it wasn't long enough to completely cover her cheeks as she ducked back into the bathroom. She reappeared a moment later with her rinsed pants on a hanger and crossed the room in front of me to suspend them over the heating unit by the window.

I smiled. "I can see your butt."

She looked over her shoulder. "You like that, don't you."

I wiggled my eyebrows. "Yeah. Very sexy."

She finished hanging the pants to dry, then winked and turned her back to me again. She wiggled that incredibly cute ass. "Wiggle-wiggle-womp."

I groaned and she teased me with a series of wiggles.

"Lucky for you," she said, "this is a double elimination tournament." She tugged her T-shirt off. "Let's see if you can win this round." She climbed onto the bed and straddled me. "Then we'll be forced to hold a playoff to determine the winner."

"Sounds like a win-win situation to me," I said happily.

I pulled into the driveway at home and sighed. The tournament was over again until next year. My team didn't win and I missed cheering next to my girl, but it was still the best tournament experience I could remember. I smiled at the memory of Haley and waking up the next morning to an empty room and the badger staring at me from the pillow next to mine. *Relax and enjoy the rest of the tournament. Sorry I can't stay,* the note said. I plucked the little guy from his spot on the dash of my truck, grabbed my duffel and went inside.

"Honey, I'm home." Her car was in the driveway, so she was here somewhere.

"Hey baby, did you have a good time?" Her muffled voice came from the laundry room.

"Probably the best tournament ever," I said, placing my little badger buddy on the kitchen counter.

"Throw your duffel in here and I'll add your dirty clothes to the ones I'm washing."

"Why don't you come out here first. I brought you a little present." I could almost see her rolling her eyes, sure that I'd brought home the hundredth free basketball T-shirt they throw out into the crowd at every tournament.

Still, she dutifully appeared and I pulled her into my arms for a long kiss.

"Wow," she said, when I released her. "I thought you'd be pouting because our team lost the final."

"Nope." I grabbed the badger and held him up. "I brought you a souvenir."

She took him and I dropped my hands lower to cup her. Yeah, I'm an ass woman, for sure. She squeezed his little paw and I palmed her butt when he growled out "wiggle-wiggle-womp."

She wiggled her eyebrows at me and I laughed, feeling so free and relaxed and loved.

"But Haley...really? That's the name you came up with?"

"She's your favorite player. You've been drooling over her all season."

"She a twenty-year-old child, and I only drool over you."

I kissed her again, then drew back and looked into those Carolina-blue eyes that could almost make me forget I'm a die-hard Duke fan. "I'm going to have to work hard to top that little role play."

She laughed. "You liked it, huh?"

I tossed my duffel into the laundry room and stripped to throw my clothes in after it. Then I winked and turned my back to her and wiggled my ass.

"Wiggle-wiggle-womp," I said, sprinting to the bedroom with her hot on my heels.

LONG DRIVE

L.C. Spoering

The drive to the airport was long enough to make my legs twitch, my foot in danger of hopping off the gas pedal at random intervals, as though it might find a way, Fred Flintstone–like, to speed us up, dash along the pavement under the car so that we met our destination that much sooner.

Early morning, the sun rose off to the left of me, making my arm appear as the desert, or untouched snow, slowly turning pink and orange and gold, inching up my limb to warm the side of my face. I tilted my head into the light and hummed with the radio, against it, my own tune in contrast to the beat from the speakers. The day was finally here.

I felt as though everything had been meticulously scheduled, turned into an orchestrated event that could fall apart with one missed step: flight delayed, baggage lost. What kind of expectations could be dashed by the carelessness of the totally ignorant? I tried not to dwell on it, parked the car in the garage and tipped my head back for one final cigarette, breathing in the smoke like I was a dragon, and it was my life force.

The giddiness lay in my stomach, curled and purring like a cat. If I was in a movie, I thought, I'd pull out a photo of her now, trace the curve of her cheek with one calloused finger, admire the slightly lopsided angle of her smile. I thought of that, before leaving the house: the photo I kept of her on the refrigerator, something enough to embarrass her. The rest of the photos, though, lay on my computer, sent over a year of emails, snapshots requested and swapped, like pen pals at childhood summer camp, SWAK written in sloppy letters over the seal of the envelope.

I ground the cigarette out in the ashtray and looked at the doors of the terminal again. I remembered the days when you could meet people at the gate and the movie scenes that came out of that, of running to planes, of waiting for a person to disembark, holding a single rose. I would meet her outside the train doors, which I tried to tell myself was the next best thing. There was still a sense of romanticism in that sort of greeting—we could be Edwardian, standing in the mists of a London evening, rather than the recycled air of a twenty-first-century airport.

I was getting ridiculous. I locked the car and hurried into the airport to check the flight times. The place smelled like floor wax and French fries, and I breathed it in like a perfume. Her flight was due in fifteen minutes, and as I walked, my brain drifted, lifted like a balloon toward the ceiling, and I hummed, again, that same purring feeling in my stomach raised to my mouth, as though emotion had a sound, as if feelings could be made into a rhythm. I cast smiles at everyone I passed, and I'm sure I looked like someone deranged: hands deep in pockets and hair a mess from fingers delved into it a few too many times. I'd agonized over my dress and then ended up in jeans. It was the way these things went, I thought—elation that turns to panic that turns transcendent.

I checked the arrival boards again. Gate A34. I could imagine her, shuffling down the aisle of the plane with the other passengers, that incredibly slow disembarkment like water slowing to a trickle. She didn't check a bag, her text said, she had everything in her carry-on. I tried to envision the contents and then stopped myself. Even I have a desire for surprise.

I hummed again and bought a cup of coffee. She didn't drink coffee, she told me early on, only tea. I had bought tea and lined up the boxes on my kitchen counter, each one another brick of anticipation that had become something like a totem, a physical path built to her arrival. She didn't like to fly, but was flying out to me. She always wore skirts. These were absolutes, and my heart clawed at the backs of my ribs in excitement. It was a new feeling, and one that was familiar, in a way. The response to her, her presence or the promise of, did this to me, like a drug that rushed to the head with the first inhale and pushed out through my veins and arteries until my extremities tingled.

I waited, holding my phone in my hand, turning it over and over against my palm as if that would change the time, would pull a message from her out of the air, plucked like a bird. I wanted her mouth, and my eyes slipped closed for just the barest of moments and I sucked in a breath, feeling the shiver work its way down my spine to settle at my lower back, wrap around my waist like arms and delve down into the cradle of my pelvis to rock there, warm water in a tub. I stood on the moving walkway and the faint tremble of the device shot to my already aching clit. I wondered how badly I'd freak out visitors if I moaned. I felt like a bottle, shaken, all the carbonation stirred with no outlet until uncapped. I needed to be uncapped.

I went as far as security allowed and stood, my forgotten coffee cupped between two hands. The airport was slowly awakening. Early flights left the place eerie and quiet, and I found I liked the atmosphere. It felt like my own anticipation colored the air, rising like clouds, and I checked the arrivals board once more. *At Gate.*

I dropped the coffee into a wastebasket and waited. I wondered if she was nervous. I knew I was not. I tasted my lips with the tip of my tongue, the flavor of lip gloss and coffee, faint tinge of tobacco.

We met on the Internet. A forum, a chat room, and those words were enough for people to roll their eyes almost immediately.

"How do you know she's not a fifty-year-old guy in diapers living in his mom's basement?" a friend asked, a variation on the same theme as everyone else. How did I indeed, of course. And there was no way I could really say it didn't matter. I knew, though, and trusted her, and her photos were always the same: blond hair, brown eyes, a slight gap between her front teeth. In those photos, she held balloons at a surprise party, a cup of tea between mittened hands at the park, wore a baseball cap in the glaring sun of a game. Her gaze was always the same, her smile crooked, as though she was never completely comfortable having a camera aimed in her direction. I loved her before I met her, and the photos were just a bonus.

I rose up on my toes and searched for her over the small surge of passengers streaming out of the terminal shuttle. It was early enough that she wouldn't be lost in the crush, but still I worried. I worried that after all this time, all the waiting, she would somehow slip past me in the crowd and we would be forever destined to be apart, to never quite meet, to never quite touch.

I had never been so dramatic in my life. I wondered what she'd done with my rational mind. I held my breath, and then there she was: same shy gaze, same unsure smile, though it was only my eyes and not the Cyclops of the camera upon her. She had a purse over one shoulder, a small suitcase in her other hand, and her toes touched when she hesitated at the gate, giving me the chance to hurry forward, push past the stragglers, and finally reach her.

"Hey, you made it," I said—not the greeting I'd really been going for. But her smile made up for it, the light behind her eyes, and she nodded with her tooth caught at the corner of her rosebud mouth.

"I made it." The same voice from over thousands of miles of Internet connection, now in person rather than over digital pathways that crackled and dropped too often.

I grinned and, without thinking, cupped her face with both hands, fingers pressing into the freckles that dotted her jaw like a spray of sand. "I'm so glad you're here."

We kissed and, after a moment, she let the bags sag to the marble floor so her hands could rest softly on my shoulders and then grasp at my neck. She had a light, sweet touch, like her lips, and my heart bounced in my rib cage once again, my blood rushing to my fingers and toes, the pit of my belly to rush between my legs, a hard, delicious ache.

The kiss broke and I curled a hand around hers, lacing our fingers together so that our palms, both damp, pressed against one another and stuck, like glue. "Come on."

She didn't budge right away, and I picked up her suitcase, pulling her closer so that our hips touched, even through the fabric of my jeans, of her skirt. She looked out of breath, flushed, and I was about to apologize when I caught the gleam in her eyes and the poise of her mouth, bottom lip pouched and still wet, glistening from our kiss.

I pulled in a breath over my own bottom lip and then smiled. "I said, come on," I told her, raising my eyebrows, though my feet were already pointing in a different direction.

I knew the path to the car; the airport was no stranger to me.

L.C. SPOERING

Instead, I led her down the long terminal under the overhead walkways and the trees, planted in the center of the airport, stretching toward the ceiling and the sunlight just filtering through the skylights. The clouds turned a sort of pink against the lightening blue of the sky. My heart pumped in my ears, and she squeezed my hand, as if she knew.

I pushed open the door to the bathroom with one hand, still pulling her along with the other. It was on the far end of the terminal and empty, and I don't know what I would have done had it not been because, quite immediately, I had her pushed up against the wall. Trapping her there with my body, I had my mouth on hers again.

It welled up from somewhere inside, and the kiss that had been something sweet out at the gate turned into one more desperate, marked by the hour driving out there, the days waiting for her flight, the months of nothing but Skype and emails.

Her bags dropped to the tiled floor and her fingers threaded in my hair, clutching at the locks I usually kept tucked behind my ears. Her fingertips were blunt and soft, her nails short but scraping over my scalp, and pressed against her, I could feel her heart thrumming in time with my own, as though they, too, were making an attempt to leap out of our bodies and clutch at each other in kind.

My knee found its way between her thighs, my foot sliding between hers to widen her stance. She came down on my thigh harder than she expected and let out a yelp-moan into my mouth, her eyes popping open and fingers grabbing more harshly at my hair.

"That flight took forever," she informed me, her voice still that shy timbre, but eyes alight with something I didn't think I'd seen before, even in photos, even in the video chats where I watched her come.

"This *year* took forever," I corrected her, lifting up onto my toe to press the firmer part of my leg to her crotch just to hear her catch her breath.

"This year," she agreed, and our mouths drove back together of their own accord, tongues tangling and teeth all but scraping. The kiss was sloppy and hard, and I kicked her suitcase in the direction of the door, an ineffectual doorstop, but I didn't dwell on it.

She wore skirts all the time, she told me once, but I liked to think this skirt was picked specifically for me, for the way it fanned out over my thigh so I could slip my fingers up under the hem with ease. Her panties were made of a slick material, soft, and when I edged my leg back down so her feet landed with a small slap on the tile floor, my hand slipped easily under the panel of fabric that covered her cunt, to that warm wetness I could practically smell.

She wiggled and let out a breath that was colored by a squeal. "Here?"

Her body dropped onto my hand, my fingers slipping over and through her crevices and folds.

"I can't wait." I pushed her more solidly against the wall, forcing her hips to meet me.

Her fingers curled at the back of my neck and her head tipped back against the wall so I could see her staring at me through slitted lids. Her lips were still parted and wet, a bruised red and purple, cheeks flushed. Even in the harsh light of the bathroom, she looked stunning, and I leaned in close as my fingers grazed her clit and bit at her small smile.

"You're all mine now," I whispered against her bottom lip.

Automatically, as if on a string, she whimpered and bore down on my hand. My fingers breached her opening with that motion and slid hard into her cunt, which contracted around me. The noise she made sounded surprised, and she rolled her head to the side to press her cheek against the blue tile wall that ran behind her, her hair scattering over her shoulder. With my free hand, I reached up and brushed it away from her face, tracing the line of her cheek. I didn't want her hiding now.

My thumb moved to her clit and swept a circle over the hard little nub, pulling a groan from her mouth. I'd dreamed of fucking her, and had told her so on more than one occasion but, as with dreams, the reality was something different, something thrilling and better, and I could feel my heart beating all over my body—in my ears and at my wrists, the arches of my feet and at the small of my back, behind my nose, even, like my blood was pulsing with every breath of hers, surging with every noise that escaped her.

Her fingers dug into my hair with a renewed grip, and she tipped her hips closer. She rocked back on her heels and then rose up on her toes, back and forth, fucking my hand in unconscious abandon. My mouth landed on her cheek, jaw, neck, bit and sucked there, and her gasps tilted another way, a little shriek, my name hissed out on a low exhale.

My pelvis felt filled with lava, with that persistent, nearly annoying, certainly needy, tingle at the apex of my sex making me fuck her harder. Her cunt grasped at my fingers, the muscles strong and eager, and I pushed into her hard, thumb rolling shapes over her clit: a circle, a star, a heart.

I could feel her orgasm rising in her, and the noise she made just before it sounded almost a little panicked. My mouth covered hers then, so she could shout against my tongue, the sound absorbed by our saliva and lips, and my hand worked her until she sagged back against the wall, shaking, gelatinous now, whimpering under my kiss.

"Finally." I sighed and leaned my forehead against hers, lips brushing against hers with my words.

She nodded and her fingers dug into my hair again, if a little weak now. "So much better when you do it," she said, a giggle in her voice. The shyness was starting to ebb off as it always did after a few minutes of conversation, after a good fuck.

I bit at her bottom lip. "Still love watching you."

She sucked in a breath. "I know." She paused. "I love you."

I rubbed our noses together, slid my hand from between her legs to pinch her thigh, and then gathered her closer to me. "Love you too." A squeeze. "Let's get you home."

The car ride, this time, was so much shorter.

DANCE FEVER

Kara A. McLeod

I glanced at my watch for the third time in fifteen minutes and frowned. The party was still going strong and showed no signs of flagging.

I sighed and considered my options. True, I was having a blast. Ever since I'd transferred squads, my former partner Rico and I didn't see much of one another, and I welcomed any opportunity to spend time with him. That his wife Paige was here as well was just frosting on the cake.

However, it was late, and I'd imbibed all the alcohol I was inclined to drink for one evening and switched to a steady stream of water some time ago. Plus I had an early appointment in the morning, which would be the beginning of a very long day for me. Perhaps it was time for me to pack it in.

"You keep looking at your watch," Rico said. "You got a hot date or something?"

I smiled ruefully. "Yup. Early start tomorrow."

Rico made a face. "Ugh. That sucks."

"Tell me about it."

"So you've got to get going?"

"'Fraid so."

Rico looked sorry to hear that, but didn't argue.

"Wait, you can't go," Paige interjected.

"Sorry, sweetie. I have an early day tomorrow. I need to get some sleep." I failed to mention that sleep had been largely elusive to me recently and that chances were the trend would continue. It seemed counterproductive.

"But…" Paige's brow wrinkled, and she was obviously struggling to come up with a reason why I should stay.

I continued to watch her in expectation, and Rico and I exchanged amused glances.

"You and Rico have to dance first," Paige proclaimed matter-of-factly.

I blinked. "What?"

Paige nodded, the sage expression on her face contrasting with the dazed look in her eyes. "Yup. You guys gotta dance. I picked a song and everything. I've been waiting."

"Paige, honey," Rico said patiently, clearly trying not to laugh. "This isn't really a dancing kind of a place."

Paige shrugged, completely unconcerned. "So? I wanna see you guys dance." Paige's gaze fell on someone standing just behind me. "Tell 'em." She put her hands on her hips and glared from the newcomer to Rico to me and back again.

I glanced over my shoulder and smirked when I realized the person Paige was ordering around was Allison, who'd just wandered into this conversation and was completely clueless as to what Paige was demanding that she tell us.

Allison looked to me for help, but I just shrugged. I was too busy battling the conflicting feelings I was having concerning her—freed from their confines by the copious amounts of alcohol I'd consumed, no doubt—to take much interest in the discussion.

"You should see these two dance," Paige told Allison, apparently tired of waiting for a response from any of us. "It is so fucking *hot!*"

Allison raised her eyebrows at me, a small, almost indulgent smile stealing over her oh-so-kissable lips. Her expression was nothing short of intrigued, and I felt a blush rising unbidden to my cheeks.

When Rico and I had been paired up together for an undercover op involving a dance club, I'd learned that as the youngest of five children with four older sisters, Rico had been enlisted as a practice dance partner from the time he could walk, and he had subsequently gained some serious moves. I'd taken my fair share of dance lessons as a kid, too, and had explored many different styles. The result of our inadvertent pairing for that assignment had been a lot of interesting dance combinations.

Rico and I quickly discovered we moved well together. We became something of a club favorite with the patrons and bartenders and eventually garnered the attention of the club's owner. The relationship we'd built with him and some of his employees led to them trusting us enough to let slip little details concerning the non-club-related activities that were occurring on the premises. Together with the information we'd gathered during independent investigation as well as tips from another confidential informant, we'd had all the probable cause we needed to get search warrants for the club and the owner's residences. After that, it was a done deal.

Rico and I hadn't had much of an opportunity to do a lot of dancing since the operation ended. On the rare occasion we did go out together, the music generally wasn't anything that would lend itself to what I would classify as actual dancing, and the atmosphere was always less than ideal. Most of our after-work outings were held at some version of an Irish pub, and who really felt comfortable doing anything remotely resembling a merengue in a place where people habitually did shots and flung darts around?

"You dance?" Allison murmured, sounding amused.

I studied her for a moment, trying to determine whether she was teasing or not. "A little."

"There's this song," Paige slurred. Clearly none of us needed to be present for this conversation. She seemed hell-bent on driving it whether we actively participated or not. "It's kind of old, but it was on the radio the other day, and the second I heard it, I thought, 'Rico and Ryan would look smokin' if they danced to that.'" She blinked at us expectantly.

"I'm not really dressed for dancing, Paige."

Paige's bleary eyes looked me up and down. "You look great."

I lifted one foot and hitched up the leg of my jeans a little. "I'll probably break an ankle in these."

"Ooh, those are cute! Where did you get them?" Paige frowned. "Wait, what did you wear on your sting?"

I tried not to smile. "I had lower heels for that. And it wasn't a sting. I'll tell you what. I'll hang out for another half hour, okay? If the song comes on, let us know. Maybe we'll dance to it."

Paige nodded happily and stumbled into Rico. She ran her hands over his chest and then threaded them behind his neck. She tilted her face up to his, wordlessly asking for a kiss. Rico's eyes danced as he eagerly complied.

Smiling wistfully, I turned to give them a moment of relative privacy and ended up face-to-face with Allison, which made my heart thud wildly out of control. I felt awkward standing next to her while Rico and Paige were putting on a genuine display of adoration, and was definitely at a loss as to what to say. For lack of any better ideas, I shoved my hands into my pockets and looked toward the bar.

My head swam and my ears rang as a feeling of déjà vu threatened to overwhelm me. I'd never been particularly suave in this type of situation, and I sure as hell didn't know how to act now.

Once upon a time, Allison and I had been a normal, happy couple. Well, sort of. But for reasons I was never able to get her to confess, she'd wanted to keep our relationship a closely guarded secret. I'd spent a lot of nights just like this one, standing next to her while feeling as though we were emotionally miles apart. And that was on good nights. More often than not, we spent the evening on opposite sides of a room, each pretending the other didn't exist, though I was always acutely aware of her presence the way you can always tell where the sun is even without looking directly at it.

At first, it hadn't bothered me. I didn't want everyone in the entire agency to know my business either. We all spend so much time together, after a while familiarity takes its toll and conversation degenerates into gossip. And when it comes to gossip, we're often worse than adolescents.

Unfortunately, as time wore on, I became less able to hide my feelings for her, to say nothing of actually being inclined to do it. I could understand her desire to avoid PDA when we were out with the work crowd, but to get pissed because I touched her lightly on the arm? Smiled at her? Tried to have a conversation with her? That, I couldn't understand. Her aversion to almost any amount of interaction with me in public did more than just anger me. It fucking hurt.

The fine line she'd expected me to walk had been extreme,

too. If I didn't pay any attention to her at all, she accused me of ignoring her and got upset. I couldn't win.

Ultimately, the entire situation became too much. For both of us. I was on edge all the time, worried that I was going to inadvertently make her mad. But underneath all that, so much more was tearing me apart. I was sad that we couldn't just be happy together. I was devastated that she seemed ashamed of us—ashamed of me. I was angry with myself for not being able to just accept her wishes, feeling as if I was pushing her to over-react. And I was pissed off at her for putting me in that situation to begin with.

In the end, we just fell apart. I think there was too much between us by that point. Too much fighting, too much resent-ment, too much pain. I couldn't see any way to fix it, and Allison clearly hadn't wanted to. She'd shattered me and never once looked back.

So here we were again, in a setting so disconcertingly familiar that I was startled to feel pangs of the old anxiety tying my stomach in knots. I hadn't known what to do years ago. What made me think I would have a better clue now?

Allison took the decision of what to do next out of my hands by resting one of hers on my forearm. The sparks her touch inflamed in me lit a path straight to all the most sensitive points of my body, and I stifled a gasp. Confused both by her actually touching me in public as well as by my own reaction, I looked into her eyes, hoping for answers.

"Relax," Allison said softly. She squeezed my arm gently before letting go.

My thoughts reeled. I hadn't meant for her to see my unease. "You're doing it again."

"Doing what?"

"That mind-reading thing. I told you before, it's creepy."

Allison chuckled. "Well, you're not that hard to read."

I sighed, mildly irritated. "For everyone?"

Allison shook her head. "I don't think so. Just for the select few who are fortunate enough to know you well."

"Oh. And you think you know me well, do you?" My tone was teasing, and I cocked my head to one side as I waited for her retort.

"Well enough to know what you're thinking about right now."

"Oh, yeah? And what's that?"

"Do I really have to say it?"

I scoffed. "You can't because you don't know."

Allison leaned in so that her lips were pressed right up against my ear, making me shiver. "You were thinking about kissing me."

My jaw dropped. That was the first time she'd acknowledged my attraction to her out loud since before we'd split up. I absolutely had not expected that. It also hadn't been remotely close to what I had been thinking.

"I was not!" My protest was vehement and a little shrill as I tried to come up with a way to convince her that she was wrong. My face was on fire.

Allison's lips quirked, and her eyes sparkled. "You are now, though, aren't you?" She blew me a playful kiss and sauntered triumphantly over to the bar, putting a little extra sway in her hips as she walked.

Game. Set. Match.

Once I'd finally recovered from the shock of her statement, which had clearly been some sort of trap, I smiled to myself. Ooh, she was so bad. She was also right, damn it all. Now that she'd brought it up, I *was* thinking about kissing her. I was also thinking about a host of other things, all of them involving my lips and her body in varying stages of undress.

Okay, I was still incredibly attracted to her. That was a given. I might not have wanted it to be, but facts were facts, and I really needed to face them. With one offhanded quip, she could still light a fire in me that threatened to rage unchecked until I was reduced to embers.

I'd been fighting that realization for days now, since Allison had arrived in New York. Despite the few fleeting looks and brief touches, I'd been convinced that she held no feelings for me beyond us being coworkers and former lovers. Dwelling on something that wasn't ever going to come to pass had seemed pointless.

Now, however, I wasn't so sure. Most people, as far as I knew, didn't say things like that to people they weren't drawn to. Well, not unless they got off on making people want them for mere sport. Which I knew Allison didn't. So part of her must still desire me. My heart stuttered at the thought, and I looked at her with new eyes as she headed back my way with another round.

Granted, the timing could have been better. Besides, wanting to go to bed and wanting to rekindle a romance were two different longings entirely. One didn't necessarily lead to the other.

How would I feel about that? If we were to fall into bed tonight—not that I was necessarily expecting us to but just hypothesizing that *if* we did—could I be content with just sex? Would I be able to handle making love to her only to have her walk unceremoniously back out of my life? I didn't think so. No, I knew that would shatter me all over again.

"Thinking about kissing me isn't supposed to make you all broody," Allison teased, handing me another water.

I shook my head, accepted the offered drink, and took a long swallow while glancing around instinctively to see whether anyone was close enough to overhear us. It wasn't like her to be so open with these types of discussions in public. Not when there were coworkers lurking around. "It's not that."

She took a sip of her gin and tonic. "What's got you so tied up in knots, then?"

I studied her for a moment, attempting to decipher the meaning behind her actions and each of the words she'd uttered from her first appearance in my office all the way up to now in a split second. It didn't work. I was still completely clueless. I didn't at all enjoy the feeling, but I accepted that for tonight at least, I was through thinking.

"I'd gotten past thinking about kissing and had moved on to contemplating other things. I was brooding because I was wondering whether it was a good idea. To be thinking about those other things."

"What other things?" Allison's tone had an air of forced innocence to it that belied the hint of passion swirling behind her gaze.

"You're a smart girl. I think you can figure that out on your own."

When she didn't reply, I fixed her with a long look, allowing her to see the desire I knew was in my eyes. If she was going to get pissed at me for it, so be it. She'd started this little game with her cheeky comment. She could damn well deal with my response. And if anger was to be hers, there wasn't anything I could do about it. Besides, she was going back to D.C. tomorrow. Surely I could withstand whatever ire she could throw my way in the next half hour or so without suffering too much damage. What more did I have to lose at this point?

Anger, however, was not what I saw on her face. Lust-tinged surprise would be a closer description. Her eyes widened just a little, and she inhaled sharply. She swallowed, and the tip of her tongue darted out to swipe across her bottom lip. The hand that came up to brush her hair back off her forehead was trembling.

"Any more silly questions?"

Mutely, Allison shook her head.

I smiled and took another sip of water to distract myself. I forced my mind to concentrate on the cool wash of the liquid as it hit my tongue and slid down my suddenly dry throat. God, I wanted to touch her. Nothing too intimate or dirty. Something small. Just a brief meeting of hands or a swift brush of fingers against the bare skin of her shoulder. I wanted it so badly that I ached. But I wasn't sure whether she'd welcome that. I didn't want to up the ante too soon.

"You need to stop looking at me like that," she warned, her voice a throaty rumble.

"Why's that?"

Inwardly, I cringed, worried I'd already gone too far. Silence reigned for so long that I was positive she wasn't going to answer, and I'd be left with nothing but the din of my wildly thudding heart for company.

Allison took another sip of her drink, drawing out my torture. "Do you remember the first day we met?"

Did I remember? Idly, I wondered which part she was referring to. The tension that had immediately built between us when we'd made eye contact for the first time? The sparks that had been the result of the first brush of her fingers against mine? The way we hadn't been able to refrain from touching one another, even innocently? Perhaps she meant the way my pulse raced each time I'd gotten so much as a glimpse of her magnificent smile. Or maybe she was talking about the way everything in my world had suddenly made perfect sense the instant our lips had touched. Truthfully, there wasn't a single second of my time with her that day that I didn't remember.

"Vividly."

Her gaze captured mine and held for a long moment. The longing teeming in her eyes made me forget how to breathe for a second. I swallowed hard and took another gulp of water in a vain attempt to dispel the dryness in the back of my throat.

"The stools over by that pool table look to be about the same height as the benches at the range, don't you think?"

I flicked a glance at the furniture in question, and my mind whirled with clear memories of our first trip to the shooting range overlaid by images of me treating her to a repeat performance in the middle of the bar for all the world to see. My already racing pulse picked up speed, and I closed my eyes as a stab of pure need shot through me.

Allison's lips brushed against my ear again, and I felt that touch acutely all over my entire body. "That's why you need to stop looking at me like that. If you don't, I can't be held responsible for what I'll beg you to do to me."

Her lips gently caressing my sensitive skin silenced the cacophony of memories rolling around inside my head and yanked me headlong back into the present. "Not up for a live sex show. Duly noted."

Allison grinned at me. "Not just yet. But I do remember someone promising me a plaid skirt once upon a time."

I laughed. "I'll see what I can do."

"This is it! This is it!" Paige's excited squeals shattered the intimate moment, and she almost knocked me down with an overly enthusiastic lunge in my direction. She tugged insistently on my arm, and I was thankful it was not the arm holding the water. That would have been messy. And I was already wet enough in other places as it was.

Paige looked from me to Allison expectantly, gleeful anticipation brimming in her eyes. I listened intently. I knew this song.

Paige had been right. It was kind of old. And it would be fun to dance to. I glanced at Rico, who shrugged.

"I'm game if you are," he said.

I held out my glass to Allison. "Do you mind?"

"Not at all." She was smiling at me in a way that made me faintly dizzy.

"Wait till you see this," I heard Paige exclaim. "My God, I just want to jump them both when they do this."

My eyes widened, and I glanced back over my shoulder to see Allison torn between laughter and intrigue. I shook my head and stepped into Rico's waiting arms. We paused a moment, getting the beat of the song before we moved. I felt the muscles in his arms tense, and instantly I realized what part of the song was coming and what he was about to do.

"Dump me on my ass, and I'll pistol whip you," I promised.

Rico just laughed. And then I was spinning, one revolution for each count the singer made. I'd caught on to his intentions just in time, too. If I hadn't been prepared for that, my legs would have tangled, and I would have gone down, probably taking him with me. Gutsy move on his part. I was a tad unsteady in heels this high as it was.

I forced myself to block out everything—the lights, the setting, the guys, the fact that I could practically feel Allison's hot gaze on my skin—and just concentrate on the beat and Rico. It didn't take long to get caught up in our familiar rhythm. The rest of the world just faded away as we moved together, and I caught myself grinning.

Rico met my eyes, and he echoed my smile before turning me again. It had been far too long since I'd been out dancing, and I had somehow forgotten how much fun it was. I made a mental note to make sure to ask Rico and Paige to go out again soon and counted myself lucky that Paige couldn't dance like this and didn't mind lending me her husband once in a while.

The song was over much too soon. Rico lifted me into his arms and spun me around as the last chords of the music faded away. The five or six guys from work who were still left in the bar broke into spontaneous applause, and Rico and I made a big show of bowing to the crowd. I laughed right along with him as we stumbled, beaming and a little breathless, back over to Allison and Paige.

Paige's grin stretched from ear to ear and her glassy eyes sparkled. "That was great, you guys." She nudged Allison. "Weren't they great?" She didn't wait for an answer as she wrapped her arms around Rico and folded him in an exuberant hug.

Allison was staring at me, something not unlike shock painted across the planes of her face. I frowned at her, puzzled.

"What?"

"I didn't know you could do that."

I shrugged and glanced away, embarrassed. I wasn't quite sure whether she was complimenting me or criticizing, so I opted to keep quiet.

"Have you always been able to do that?"

"For as long as I can remember."

"I've never seen you do that before."

"Well, no, you wouldn't have."

She waited for me to look at her before she spoke. "It was *very* hot."

A sharp stab of desire cut straight through me at the heat in her tone. "It's even hotter when I do it with someone I'm actually attracted to."

She was quiet for a long moment and something intense and almost primitive flickered in her eyes. "Could you teach me?"

"Definitely." I listened to the song that was currently playing. Nope. This wouldn't work. The beat wasn't right, and I wasn't quite able to move against it. It would be too difficult. Too distracting. I'd feel compelled to try to make my motions go with the tempo. Maybe the next one.

"Let's go." Allison's voice held more than a hint of a command, and underneath there was a slim thread of passion.

I shook my head. "Not now."

Allison's expression was awash with something not unlike hurt. She set her jaw. "Okay."

Unthinkingly, I rested one hand on her bare forearm. "I'm not a very good lead. I haven't had that much practice at it." I sketched a vague gesture in the air, indicating the song that was playing. "I won't be able to dance to this, let alone teach anyone else how to. I'm not proficient enough to ignore the beat. Rico might be able to do it, but if you want me, we'll have to wait for another song."

Realization dawned on Allison's face followed by a tender sort of smile.

"No, I meant let's leave."

"Oh." A pause. "I thought you wanted me to teach you to dance."

When Allison shook her head, I was mesmerized by the sway of her dark hair brushing the tops of her bare shoulders. "I do. But not here."

I colored, chastising myself for forgetting that we had an audience, as was so often the case when I was in her presence. She wouldn't want them to see us doing something as intimate as dancing. She was right, of course. There was no need to fuel their fantasies. Besides, there was no guarantee that after five seconds of moving with her in my arms while she was staring at me with that hungry look on her face, I wouldn't ravage her on the spot, audience and probable jail time be damned.

"Oh. Right. Sorry." I hesitated for a second, thinking, and

then it hit me what she'd just said. She wanted us to leave. Together.

I gaped at her. Her blatant desire confused me. Even when we'd been a couple, she'd never wanted anyone to see us leaving a party together. We'd always had to leave separately with at least thirty minutes between our departure times, regardless of the fact that we were going to end up spending the night in each other's arms. I hesitated, not wanting to make the wrong assumption.

Allison smiled at me again, probably reading my uncertainty loud and clear, and extended a hand to me. Tentatively, I reached out and took it. One night wouldn't be enough, but it might be a new beginning. She threaded her fingers through mine and started to pull me toward the door. I stopped her with a light tug, and she turned around, her expression part bewilderment and part irritation. I squeezed her hand.

"Just give me a second to say good-bye to Rico and Paige."

Relief flickered in Allison's eyes, and she nodded once.

I hurriedly said my good-byes and floated back over to Allison, heart pounding and a flutter of nervousness tickling my insides.

Tenderness blossomed on Allison's gorgeous face as she looked at me and once again offered me her hand. She always could read me better than anyone on the planet, which could be a blessing or a curse, depending on the situation. Tonight it was definitely the former. I smiled at her as I took her hand and allowed her to lead me out the door and into the night.

COOLING DOWN, HEATING UP

Dena Hankins

I use the ribbed cotton of my tank top to dry the skin under my tits. A bra would soak up some of the sweat, but I can't bear one thread more than the top and my underwear. I'm sitting on the floor, leaning against the fieldstone fireplace in our 180-year-old farmhouse. Never thought the fireplace would be the spot in the house.

The fan squeaks a bit, way up in the high ceiling. I'll have to fix that when it's not a million degrees. The blades pour humid air over me like a warm river.

Hennie's flushed, lying flat on her back in a cotton slip she made herself. It's got thin lines of lace, top and bottom, and she scratches at her thigh where the lace tickles. She wiggles within reach, hunting a cooler spot on the wooden floor, and I poke her hip with my big toe. She groans. "I love you, sweetheart. Don't touch me."

I laugh.

The hills outside Chapel Hill, North Carolina, sport more

than one lovely old house. Ours has little in the way of grounds—
the fields had been sold long before we came around. We've
owned it three years now, moved in on our eighth anniversary.
Still getting bruised and blistered working on it, but that's just
part of owning an old home. Our bedroom is straight out of the
nineteenth century, except we made the dressing room into a
bathroom. We updated the kitchen but left the cupboards. The
old plumbing complains and we replace what we have to.

Mostly, we restore what we can and live without plenty. Like
air-conditioning.

"Hennie, I think it's time."

My lover smiles without opening her eyes. "Gettin' itchy?"

"Mmm-hmm."

Hennie sits up with a whoosh and blinks like she's light-
headed. Her slip's wet where she was lying on it. Her tits are
bare under the thin cotton and her nipples are soft, nearly flat in
the heat. "Want to make reservations or pack?"

I lever myself to my feet and wish I hadn't. "I'll pack."

Hennie laughs. "You're sweet, but I was joking. Get on the
computer and I'll put together an overnight bag."

I lean over and give Hennie my hand. We both groan at
the sticky feeling as I pull her upright. Pressing my lips to hers
without touching anywhere else, I mumble against her mouth,
"You're the one for me."

"I'd better be." Her grumpy tone makes me smile and she
pulls away. Slogging through the dank air, she heads up the
stairs to our bedroom on the second floor. Her voice fades as
she gripes, "I still say we should have a summer bedroom downstairs. We can put a bed in the piano parlor and…"

My face settles into the expression Hennie calls "mulish." I
consider that an insult and refuse to cop to it. I love our bedroom
and won't give it up for anything. A smile breaks through. Actu-

ally, I will give it up tonight for that most modern of conveniences.

We're driving away less than an hour later and pull up to the chain motel a half hour after that. After checking in, we drive around the back and park in front of the door to our room for the night.

Hennie slides the key card into the reader and shoves against the seal made by the weather stripping. She gasps and calls out, "It's already cold in here!" The delight in her voice is worth the sixty dollars we just dropped.

Holding the bag, I lock the car doors and follow her into the room. The temperature drops at the door and I shiver hard. Hennie's inspecting the room—opening drawers, checking out the bathroom. Reminds me of a dog sniffing new territory when she does that, though I'd never make the mistake of saying so. She starts the shower and yells, "Good pressure."

The shower doesn't stop. She must have decided to jump right in. Would she want something to wear afterward? I'll probably ruin a surprise if I open the bag, so I decide against getting clothes out for her. Maybe we won't wear anything until it's time to check out.

Water hits the wall and the shower curtain, the sound modulating as she moves. I picture her turning under the spray, cupping her hands and letting the cool water overflow down her chest.

I can't stay all sticky while she's getting so clean.

Down with my shorts, off with my underwear. The tank top droops, heavy with my sweat, and the chilling fabric draws another shiver from me as I pull it over my head. Damn. The cold is almost as uncomfortable as the heat.

In the cold, though, we can get close.

I push open the door to the little bathroom and it stops against the shower/tub combo. Hennie's slip is limp on the floor and I catch my first sight of her in the vanity mirror across from the shower.

Her deep curves make my insides tighten. Through the translucent plastic shower curtain, she has the mysterious proportions of a goddess. Her heavy hips and solid thighs taper to strong calves and small feet, while above…ah, above.

Hennie's breasts curve away from her ribs, lower than they were when we first stripped for one another. We attacked each other that night with the lights out. Not for shyness, but because we were in such a hurry that we forgot to turn them on.

Since then, Hennie has put on thirty, maybe forty pounds. Her breasts are heavier, her ass more padded. Her waist still has that delicious curve and her face barely shows a difference, but she looks so much more womanly to me. As a girl, she charmed me. Now I am devoted to the woman she's become.

Physically, I've always been a tit woman. I love a shapely ass, but it's big, soft tits that catch my attention when I'm supposed to be driving. When I'm shopping for groceries. When I'm ordering a meal. I love large, pillowy breasts.

Hennie's were unreal when we met—high and too firm to make deep cleavage. In my opinion, they've gotten better. They've softened, gained a deeper under-curve and, in the right bra, they push together for some jaw-dropping cleavage. It's not just me—everyone notices.

"Are you coming in or are you going to stare all night?"

I grin. "I'm doing more than staring tonight. It's been two weeks since it's been cool enough to lick your pussy, let alone fuck you." I push the curtain back and our eyes meet. "How's the shower?"

My pussy thumps when she steps sideways, letting the water sluice over her tits. "Invigorating."

"Just what I wanted to hear."

"Come on in, then."

The sultry look she gives me is hotter than the weather outside our motel room. I step over the lip of the tub and take the motel soap from her hands. She turns away while I build up a good froth. Reaching out, I slick my hands across her shoulders and sigh.

My libido doesn't disappear, but the familiar happiness of touching Hennie—scratching her back lightly, gripping the muscles of her shoulders and squeezing them in my hands—this overwhelms my lust with tenderness. We have time to be fierce with one another. First I just want to get close.

Hennie hums and tips her head back when I slide up behind her. Shower spray wets my front and I bring my tits and belly up against her soapy back. I slide my arms around her waist and fold her close.

My love likes to pretend that I am the horndog in the relationship, but she's the one who starts sliding her ass on my thighs. She's the one who lifts my hands to cup her tits and grabs the back of my neck over her shoulder. She acts like I'm the one who gets itchy and needy, but Hennie's desire burns and demands, where mine tends to glow. If I'm an ocean swell, she's that wave from *The Perfect Storm*.

"I love you," I breathe in her ear. I nibble the outer curve and suck her earlobe between my teeth. Moments like this, I'm glad I'm taller than she is. I can see her tits mounded in my palms while I run my teeth down the muscle in her neck. The taste of cheap soap makes my nose wrinkle and I let the shower rinse my mouth.

I focus on her nipples. Hennie says they're not very sensitive, but to me, they're perfect. She can take a lot of sensation. I like tugging on them hard, twisting them, gnawing and sucking. It sends me over the edge to have them in my mouth, and some

of our strangest sex positions have resulted from my desire for
Hennie's tits.

She asked me once what I'd do if she got breast cancer and
had them chopped off. I teared up and she got pissed before I
could pull it together. I wasn't crying over some damn breast
tissue, though. I freak out when she gets a splinter. I don't know
how I'd handle a major illness like cancer. Can't stand to think
about it. I hope we age well and die together in our sleep.

Hennie must feel my change of mood, me thinking about
sickness and old age, because she turns in my arms and hugs me
tight. She slides a hand into my spiky hair and pulls my head
down to her shoulder. I squeeze her and marvel at the compli-
cated swell of emotion—desperate love, warm affection, a hint
of future sadness born of my need for her. Under all that, though,
the slippery body of my lover stokes my lust.

"Finish your shower, but don't come out until you holler."
Hennie gives the order, knowing I'll bristle at her tone and get
excited at the same time. She turns around under the spray for a
final rinse and steps out.

I soap up and let the water run over me, warm water over
cool skin. Been taking cold showers for a couple months, and a
warm shower is a strange treat. Cold feels good, don't mistake
me, but it don't relax a body.

I scrub my body dry—Hennie tells me to pat, but I like the
scratching—and tug the locks over my eyebrows into a disarray
that I hope is sexy.

"Ready for me, honey?" I'm turning the doorknob as I yell.

"Come and get it," my lover growls.

I step out of the bathroom and suck in a breath. My turn, is
it?

Hennie stands in front of the heavy drapes, stroking the dark
blue dildo in her harness. The straps follow the curve of her

hips. Her hair curls around the edges of the backing pad and her belly swells gently above. The dildo is long and not very wide. I raise an eyebrow and meet her challenging look. "It's been a while," I say, by way of a warning.

"I'm feeling patient. It's not the only dildo I brought, though."

We have a few dildos we use in our harnesses. She's wearing the one we use for butt-play, and I turn my attention to my body. Clenching my sphincters and releasing them, I feel good—clean and clear, warming up to the idea of getting fucked. It's not my usual role, but Hennie's excited and that decides me.

"Let's see how it goes."

Hennie sends me her sly "got what I wanted" smile. We meet at the foot of the bed and push close, kissing deeply and squeezing the dildo between our bellies. I press the sides of her breasts with my upper arms while stroking my hands along the waist strap of the harness.

Hennie strokes my neck and shoulders, pressing her thumbs along my collarbones. I pull away and she gives me a little push so I land on the bed, on top of the damp towel she laid out from her shower. I catch myself, half-reclined with my hands braced on the bed behind me, and Hennie attacks.

My elbows fold under her weight and my breathing stops altogether with her nipple in my mouth. She thrusts the dildo against my belly, straddling me, giving me the writhing armful that gets me hot. She knows the buttons and she's pushing them all as though we're going for a quickie in a park. I reach down, but the bulk of her gorgeous ass prevents me from finding her cunt from behind.

With a whimper—the least butch sound I make—I burrow my hand between our bodies and past the dildo and harness. Slippery, swollen and hot. My love makes fists and pounds them on the bed, determined that I will not distract her, determined not to let me flip her so that she gets fucked first. She pushes her ass upward, out of my reach, and pulls her nipple out of my mouth.

"Not this time," she says, looking like an angry schoolmarm. "You fucking lie there."

I bump my hips up at her. Hennie falls back on top of me and laughs. She never does stay mad for long. She scoots down and parts my legs. The dildo bumps against my cunt and I squirm again. She puts a hand on my chest for stability and uses the other to open me up. The dildo slides a tiny ways into my cunt. I'm wet enough to slick that silicone up just fine.

Miniature thrusts and a thumb on my clit hood frustrate me, but I know she's doing it for my own good. Only way to put me into the zone is to tease me. I can come, no problem, but it's usually minor muscle spasms. For the full-body clench and release, I have to get to a much higher level of need.

Hennie's looking at my cheeks, watching me lick my lips. She presses down on my rib cage and watches my nipples harden. The calculating way she manipulates my clit, rubbing above and to each side without touching it, makes me stretch my arms up and grab for the headboard.

But we're not in our bed. My fingers scrabble against veneer and I settle for a pillow, grabbing it between my hands and wishing I had something to pull against.

Hennie is satisfied that I'm with her. She hates it when I let her fuck me, but there's no connection. She says I may as well just masturbate when I'm like that, and she's not wrong. Right now, though, it's Hennie's touch and Hennie's plan that's ratcheting my body tighter and tighter.

She slides her knees up, one at a time, shoving my legs wide and draping them over her thighs. Kneeling, she leaves the dildo in my cunt, where it teases me with hints of pleasure without being wide enough to stretch me the way I love. She gloves one hand, lubes up both and slides the gloved one below the dildo.

Her fingers slip over the tiny folds around my asshole and dance around the ring of muscle holding it closed. Slipping in the lube, her fingers press and massage that ring until I feel it happen. I start to open up.

Meeting my eyes, she dallies until I exhale. Her teasing thumb presses my clit finally and then, as I arch up into that touch, she slips her index finger inside my ass. I can't help the clench that follows. It's not a rejection. It's a plea to stay.

Gently rubbing me all around, she focuses on easing my tight-ness. I do my best to help out with deep breathing, but Hennie doesn't want me too relaxed. She keeps stroking my clit, but only in ways that don't, won't get me off. Eventually, my eyes slide shut and my hips start to wander.

That's the moment Hennie's been waiting for. When I move into hungry receptivity, she pulls the dildo from my cunt and slides it a tiny bit into my ass. The hand on my clit goes still and then her palm presses against it, giving me something to rub on without distracting me from the deep give of my ass opening to her. Took a lot of fucking for her to pinpoint the moment when the clit stimulation needed to stop, but she nailed it this time.

I love this moment. I can feel muscles slacken inside my body, muscles I'm not aware of on a day-to-day basis. She slides in and my insides rearrange to accommodate her. Fresh lube cools the dildo and is warmed by friction. When she stops pressing, I open my eyes.

"It's working." She presses harder against my clit as she speaks.

"Oh, yeah."

I lie on my back in an unfamiliar room, with an over-bleached motel towel under my impaled ass and goose bumps covering my body. The strangeness of our surroundings excites me, but not as much as the woman between my legs. Hennie looks abstracted, focused on the feedback she gets from the hand wrapped around the dildo. Her hips are still and she manipulates the dildo in tiny circles with her hand, watching my ass tighten and soften in response. Her intense attention is all for my body, and my body gives her what she wants.

"I think you're ready." Hennie looks up into my face, checking in.

I nod, opening my mouth to agree. A moan escapes when she pulls the dildo from my ass. Hungry to get it back, I scramble to turn over and present my ass, high and ready for her.

She makes me wait. She drifts up close behind me and slides her knees between my thighs. She lays the dildo's length between my cheeks and thrusts slowly, the slick silicone rubbing against the hot softness of my asshole. A cool deluge strikes and I flinch. Hennie laughs and rubs the lube around my asshole with the dildo, then angles it down for me.

I back down on it, gobbling it up, filling myself up and then slowing down so I can take more. It's a very long dildo and, in this position, Hennie can get close enough to give me every inch. I thrust my ass onto it a bit at a time, moaning at the depth of my penetration.

When I get all the way down on it, I push against Hennie's thighs with mine and press my asscheeks into her hips. Shaking and jerking, so close to coming, I reach for my clit but she says, "No, not yet."

I almost sob, but she starts thrusting and my attention turns. Slide and slap, and she pushes her weight into my ass. She wants me to brace so I won't slide across the bed. On my knees with my ass high and my shoulders low, I grip the bedspread in hopes it'll keep me in position.

We're both fucking now, slamming into each other hard and bouncing back, just to slam together again. It's not fast, but it's relentless and we keep it up until my grip fails and I slide forward. Hennie grabs my hips then and pulls my ass into her. I reach down for my clit and she doesn't stop me. That turns me on even more, because it means she knows how worked up I am.

My mind is clouded, dislocated. I am thinking with my gut. My clit is enormous and so is Hennie's dildo in my ass. I reach inside my cunt to feel it move. The end strokes my fingers through the thin tissue that separates one hole from the other and I have my face and chest pressed into the bed with both hands on my cunt now. Hennie is chanting, "Come for me, baby. Come for me." I'm rubbing my clit and filling my cunt. Hennie is fucking my ass so smoothly that in and out feel the same and the orgasm builds from the deepest part of me that she touches, disintegrating my flesh and replacing it with pure energy.

When the pulses slow and subside, my body re-forms around the sensation of Hennie pulling her dildo from my ass. She slips to the side, running one hand down my back, then removes the harness. While I'm still dazed, reeling from being discorporate with pleasure, Hennie turns me over.

I flop over gladly, my ass still pulsing, and take a deep breath. Good thing, too, because Hennie's pussy covers my mouth, lips held open by her slick fingers. The scent and texture of her becomes part of my lingering orgasm and I lap at her slowly. Hennie is too far gone for that, though, and she shoves her clit at my tongue.

I'm buried and helpless under her, but she only needs me to keep my tongue curled and my lips pursed. She fucks me again, this time with her clit in my mouth, climbing so quickly to orgasm that she must have been close when I came. She grabs the fake headboard in front of her and the bed pounds the wall from her jagged thrusts until she keens, a high, thin sound that means it's holding off, that the orgasm she's chasing is just beyond her reach. I add a flick of my tongue to the end of her movement and she convulses above me, belly quaking and tits shivering.

By the time her cries have lowered in pitch, I have my wits about me again. I love this woman and she has given me so much. When she gets off me, still moaning, I slip off the bed and grab the bag.

Sure enough, she also packed my harness and the fat dildo she loves so much. I strap it on. She's done all the work so far, but now I'm ready to break a sweat. Why not? We've got air-conditioning.

LITTLE BIT OF IVORY

JL Merrow

She's got perfect skin. That's what I remember most about her, when we're apart. Perfect skin, the color of new ivory. Long, long limbs and crazy hair, all piled up on her head as if she wasn't tall enough already, the bitch.

(I don't mean that spitefully, by the way. I love her.)

She never lets that hair tumble around her shoulders when we're out together. Not when she's out without me, either—and she's out too often without me, has to be in her job. She travels, you see. All over the world, charming people (men) with her smile, her witchy green eyes. Seducing them into giving her love tokens, a name on a dotted line.

(I'd give her my name, if she asked for it. Or take hers, if that was what she wanted.)

Me? I sit at home, and I wait. I tap my fingers, and words flow out, although the effect is little even after much labor.

(If I told her that, she'd laugh and call me her own dear Jane. I do love to see her laugh.)

But then she comes home to me, when my shoulders are stiff from typing and her hair's just beginning to droop. I meet her at the door (kick the junk mail out of the way first, should have tidied, too late now) and put my arms around her neck. She smiles that smile that makes her eyes go brighter, that shows the lines around the corners. (They're mine, those lines. I was there for all of their births.) It softens when my hands creep up to take out the pins, the clips, all that holds back the avalanche of burnished copper.

Her hair cascades, and her whole body relaxes, shudders. "Mmm," she says. "Missed you."

"Missed you more," I tell her (it's true). "Hungry?"

She darkens her eyebrows when she's working. Thinks they're too pale. But they're perfect, just like the rest of her, and when one quirks up I want to kiss it (it's a bugger being short). "Had a sandwich on the train. I'll keep."

"No, you won't," I tell her, pulling her by the hand. Kicking the door shut behind her.

It's only seven paces down the hall to the bedroom (I might have measured it, once). It takes us seven ages to get there. Her coat falls to the floor, an early casualty. Her shoes seem to have walked off by themselves. (They're black patent, wicked heels. I'm sure they could do a deal all on their own, if she'd let them.)

I kiss her, tasting mint and ChapStick. (She knows I love to see her in lipstick. She also knows I don't love the taste of it. I imagine her now, taking it off on the train. Moisturizing her lips again. Pressing them together, then checking in the mirror she keeps in her bag to make sure she's perfect. Was there a touch of sweat on the brow of some paunchy, middle-aged businessman sitting opposite, sneaking a glance on the way home to his disillusioned wife?)

Her tongue darts between my lips. Shy, tentative. (Oh, it's a liar, that tongue.) I meet it with mine, relearn the contours of her mouth. She's soft, so soft, where I press her to me. Her breasts, smaller than mine, don't need much support. When I knead one with my hand, I can feel her hard nipple through the thin material. I shiver and have to pull at her top. "Off," I tell her, and she laughs but pulls it off anyway.

(I take mine off too. There's no sense in wasting time.)

Her bra's pretty, but it's got to go. I unhook it gently. Cherry red nipples tease me, so I bend to taste one. So sweet and hard, and I can feel heat rising in my core, just as if it was my own breast being suckled. She moans, her hand reaching for my breast, slender fingers sliding into the cup of my bra. When she squeezes my nipple, I feel like I'll explode.

I reach around to the fastening of her skirt. Undo it and help it over those flaring hips. She's wearing stockings, black nylon held up with lace, the contrast stark with the pale perfection of her skin. I hook my thumbs into her panties and ease them down, leaving her bare but for her stockings.

"So beautiful," I murmur. I don't remember getting to my knees. I nuzzle into the fiery hair at her groin, all neatly trimmed (she used to wax, but I like her better like this so now she doesn't bother). She shudders, and I hold her tight as I lick her lips. She tastes of musk, and want, and *mine*.

"On the bed," I say, and she lies down, naked but for her stockings, her suspenders and her smile. One leg bent, the other straight, and I can see all of her, all her beauty.

"Time you got those jeans off," she says, and I scramble to obey. (Sometimes she likes the feel of rough denim against her skin. Today isn't one of those times.)

I kneel between her spread thighs and run my hands over her hips, her waist, her breasts. "Tease," she says. I know what she wants.

I circle her opening with my finger, teasing her lips and her clitoris. There's a flush of pink on my ivory canvas now, and her breasts rise and fall with her quickened breath. I push my finger inside her and her head falls back, her hair a waterfall of flames.

"More," she breathes. I add another finger, work them in and out. She's slick, warm and welcoming, her inner walls caressing me. I add a third finger. "More," she demands.

Four fingers. I add some lubricant and go cautiously now. I don't want to hurt her. (And she loves it when I tease.) My fingers still inside her, I bend over to kiss her breast, to tease her nipple with my tongue, my teeth. She groans, her body shaking. I brush her clitoris with my thumb.

Her hands push at my shoulders. "Not yet. I need all of you." (I know what she means.)

I suck hard on her nipple, bringing it to a reddened, swollen peak. Then I leave it alone, for now. Squeezing my hand as small as I can, I let my thumb slip inside her. Her hips jerk up.

"Yes. *More*."

Between my legs, I feel like I'm on fire. I push into her some more. So wet, so hot, she pulls me in. Slowly, so slowly, I watch my hand disappear inside her. She shudders and groans. "*Yes*."

I move my hand—quick little thrusts, just how she likes it. Her slender fingers scrabble and clutch at the sheets.

"More?" I ask. (I already know the answer.)

"God, yes! *Now*."

I lick the thumb of my free hand and gently brush her clitoris. She arches, crying out, and clenches around my fist. Strong, rippling contractions squeeze me, caress me. She comes and comes, leaving me slick with her juices. When she pushes at my shoulders again, I slide my hand out of her (slowly, so slowly; I don't want to leave her). She pulls me up to kiss me, her tongue now honest, demanding, invading. Her heart beats fiercely against my breast.

"God, I feel properly welcomed home," she says, her voice breathy and broken.

I nod. "Then my work here is done."

She laughs. "Mine's not." My pulse quickens as she rouses orgasm-languid limbs and slithers down the bed. "Lie back."

"And think of England?"

"Bitch. Think of me." (She knows I always do.)

I gasp as her warm breath hits my groin. Her tongue's turned wicked now, teasing as it tastes. My flesh tingles at its approach and bursts into flame at its touch. She stokes my fires with practiced skill. (What would the men in suits think now if they saw her, I wonder? Would faces flush, would hands creep into boxer shorts?) Her fingers on my hips steady me, write their own Braille across my skin. (I'll read it later, with love.)

There's a bed beneath me. I know this. Wrinkled sheets and a pillow under my head. The air in the flat is cool. I feel none of it. All I feel is her: her tongue, her hands. The ecstasy she spins out of straw. I want to paint her with words, my little bit of ivory, but my brush is fine, so fine, and all I have is pure sensation. Wordless, I cry out as she takes me to the peak and carries me over in her arms.

My limbs tangle with hers. I'd tie that knot so tight, if I could, that no one would ever be able to undo it.

And then I'd pull on the trailing thread and let it all unravel, let her go.

Just for the pleasure of having her come back home to me.

A ROYAL ENGAGEMENT

Nell Stark

Her Royal Highness Princess Alexandra Victoria Jane—better known to her subjects as Sasha—peered around the stage and into one corner of the Throne Room. Strobe lights illuminated a small cluster of people centered on one of her cousins and his date. She sighed in frustration, even as she waved to them. Where on earth had Kerry gone?

Turning in a slow circle, she surveyed the stateroom turned nightclub. Her brother Arthur and his wife Ashleigh were up onstage, dancing with a knot of their closest friends. The newlyweds had changed into evening attire for this reception, and Sasha had no doubt that the tabloids would be thrown into paroxysms of joy at their fairy-tale perfection. Ashleigh looked stunning in her floor-length white evening gown, and Arthur had ditched his Royal Air Force uniform for a tuxedo.

Sasha watched as he twirled his wife expertly in time to the music. They looked so happy. They *were* so happy. For years, she had secretly despaired of ever falling in love, not to mention finding someone to share her life. Thankfully, Kerry had changed all that, and now Sasha was ready to take the next step. But first, she had to find her.

After several more minutes of hunting, Sasha saw her standing near one of the tables set around the periphery of the room. She was sharing it with Sasha's sister Lizzie and a few of her Cambridge friends, and as Sasha watched, Kerry tipped her head back and laughed. Her wavy red hair was artfully mussed, and her silver tux showed off both the breadth of her shoulders and the swell of her breasts.

Sasha hurried over and slipped one arm around Kerry's waist. "You're looking quite handsome tonight, Ms. Donovan."

"Your Royal Highness." Kerry's eyes twinkled. "What an unexpected pleasure."

"Unexpected?" Sasha arched one eyebrow. "You should always expect me."

"No one expects the Spanish Inquisition," quipped a clearly tipsy Lizzie, which set Kerry to laughing again.

"Nerds. The lot of you, nerds." Sasha turned her face up to Kerry's for a swift kiss. "I'm sorry I've had to spend so much time away today."

"Don't apologize. Maid of honor is a big job." Kerry pulled her closer and said quietly, "Everything okay? You seem a little tired."

"I'm fine." Sasha rested her cheek against Kerry's shoulder as they whispered. "The day went off well, I think. That's all that matters."

"You should feel pleased." Kerry kissed her again. "And I meant what I said earlier—your speech was amazing."

"You're biased."

"No. Just honest."

Sasha pulled back to meet her eyes. It was the same response

Kerry had given the night they'd met, in the moments before their first kiss. The kiss that had changed everything. Suddenly, Sasha resented every other person in the room. "I've had enough of speeches. I just want to spend time with you."

"Shall we take a walk? Get out for a little while?" Kerry looked toward the stage. "I don't think the party will slow down anytime soon."

"That sounds perfect." She turned to her sister. "We're going to take some fresh air."

Lizzie narrowed her eyes. "You're not running off to—"

"Hush." Sasha embraced her before she could finish the sentence. "We'll be back. Keep the dance floor warm."

She tugged at Kerry's hand but was forced to wait until she had exchanged cheek-kisses with Lizzie. Over the past several months, Kerry had developed strong relationships with both of Sasha's siblings. She talked football with Arthur and sat between them in their box at Manchester United games. She talked literature and history with Lizzie and had gone over to Cambridge once to support her at a debating competition.

Now, as they made their way through the crowd in search of freedom, Sasha felt her anticipation grow. Tomorrow she would formalize Kerry's place in her family. In the morning, they would all retreat to Balmoral Castle in Scotland for a few more days of private celebration before Arthur and Ashleigh embarked on their honeymoon. Once they had settled in, Sasha planned to invite Kerry to ride with her into the mountains, as they had done on their first real date. This time, in addition to producing breakfast at the ruins, she would produce a ring.

"Let's walk along the park." Kerry interrupted her reverie. "If Ian will let us, of course."

The throng that had gathered outside the palace for the nuptials that morning had since dispersed to their own celebrations in pubs and homes across the city, making Sasha's protection officer amenable to their plan. He followed them from a discreet distance as they strolled hand in hand along the mostly deserted sidewalk. The light breeze blowing through the trees felt wonderful on her face after the heat of the party.

"I still can't believe Father let us turn the Throne Room into a club."

"That was a brilliant idea, and a smash hit. I heard loads of people talking about it." Kerry squeezed Sasha's hand. "Are you cold? Want my jacket?"

"I'm fine. But thank you." Kerry's solicitousness always made her feel warm inside. Cherished. "You would have made a perfect Knight of the Round Table, you know."

Kerry laughed. "If Arthur ever decides to bring back that tradition, maybe I'll apply for a seat."

They walked on for a while, chatting about their favorite parts of the ceremony and afternoon luncheon, until Sasha realized they were crossing the street. "Where are you taking me?"

"We're almost at Parliament." Kerry gestured toward the imposing façade. Big Ben's face was especially bright this evening under the light of a nearly full moon. "Since we're in the neighborhood, I thought we might duck into Westminster Hall for a minute."

Since the beginning of the summer, Kerry had been involved in a project to renovate the oldest part of Westminster Palace. Sasha had no idea why she had chosen this moment to show off her work, but she certainly wanted to be supportive. "I'd love to see how it's coming along."

On their way into the palace, they met three different pairs of security guards, all of whom were very happy to let them pass once they'd had a good look at Sasha. Several of them also knew Kerry by name. The last of the guards were positioned directly in front of the hall, and they stepped aside with a murmured, "Your Royal Highness."

Kerry took a key from her pocket and opened the lock on the thick chain binding the doors together. She threaded the links through the handles and wound the chain around her arm before handing it to the nearest guard. And then, with a grin over her shoulder, she gave the doors a strong push. They parted slowly to reveal the hall that had once been the epicenter of the English monarchy's power.

"Shall we?" Kerry extended her arm, beckoning Sasha over the threshold. As the doors swung shut behind them, Sasha took the opportunity to survey the space as she'd never done before. Always impressive, it seemed much larger when empty. She looked up at the ornate wooden roof with its arched trusses that marched the length of the hall. Moonlight filtered through the large window overlooking the dais at the far end, creating a shimmering pool of light in the center of the raised platform.

"Follow me." Kerry gently tugged at their joined hands.

"What sort of roof is that called again?" Sasha asked as she was led down the center aisle.

"It's a hammer-beam roof. Richard II had it built in the late fourteenth century. We've had to reinforce a few sections, but it's nearly finished." Kerry pointed out a scaffold that had been erected along part of one wall.

"I heard your president address Parliament here a few years ago."

"Did he do a good job?"

"I'm afraid I didn't pay close attention." Sasha felt a twinge of guilt for her rebellious past. She had felt like such an outsider in her family until Kerry had helped her see where she fit.

"I bet he was nervous. Come on, let's go stand where he did."

"Oh? Do you have presidential aspirations?" Sasha meant

it as a joke—mostly. Sometimes she worried that Kerry would become homesick for her native land, or sacrifice some excellent career opportunity in the States to remain with her in the U.K.

"Hardly." Kerry made a face. "What a thankless job. Besides, all my aspirations are on this side of the pond." They reached the dais, and she gestured toward the stairs. "After you."

As soon as she had climbed up, Sasha found herself enveloped by the silvery spotlight created by the moon. She spun in a slow circle, taking in the entirety of the hall. An anticipatory hush pervaded the space, as though the wooden timbers themselves were waiting for something. Sasha turned to face Kerry…and found her down on one knee, hand outstretched, a ring nestled in the center of her palm. She gasped.

"Alexandra Victoria Jane." Kerry's voice shook slightly, and as Sasha watched in stunned silence, she moistened her lips with the tip of her tongue. "I've fallen more deeply in love with you than I ever thought possible. Before I met you, I didn't know enough to even dream of a romance like this. There is nothing I want more than the chance to make you happy every day for the rest of our lives." She had to pause to catch her breath, but her gaze never left Sasha's. "Will you marry me?"

Sasha could barely think over the roaring in her ears, but as she stared down at Kerry, one thing became clear. This whole plan—leaving the reception, their walk along the park, turning in to the palace—had been premeditated. Orchestrated. Kerry had brought her here expressly to propose. Sasha couldn't believe this was happening.

"No!"

Kerry rocked backward as though she'd been physically struck, and her face began to crumple before she ducked her head. Only then did Sasha realize exactly what she had said, and in horror, she sank to the floor, mindless of the dust.

"Yes! I mean yes! Yes, of course I'll marry you." She cupped Kerry's face and forced her to look up, wanting to slap herself when she saw the tears shimmering in those blue depths. What a bloody idiot she was.

"Yes?" Kerry's voice cracked. "Are you sure?"

Tenderly, Sasha raised her thumbs to wipe away the two tiny droplets that had escaped the corners of her eyes. "Yes. I want to marry you more than...than anything."

"Then why did you say no?"

Sasha leaned forward to press their lips together as she thought of how to reply. If she told the truth, she would ruin her surprise. But on the other hand, she had almost just ruined Kerry's beautiful proposal.

"Because tomorrow, I'm going to offer *you* a ring."

Kerry frowned. "You are?"

"Yes. I have a plan involving scones, horses and the Scottish Highlands. Ian is in on it." Sasha stroked Kerry's cheekbones. "And now you've gotten there first."

To Sasha's immense relief, Kerry let out a small laugh. "Really?"

"Truly. I'm so sorry that 'no' leapt out of my mouth. I was just in shock that you'd managed to beat me to the punch."

Finally, Kerry smiled—that wide, open smile reserved only for her. "I'm precocious, remember?"

"How could I forget?" Sasha kissed her again. "Can you forgive me?"

"There's nothing to forgive."

They knelt together on the dais, Sasha searching Kerry's eyes until she was sure no sign of pain lingered. "May I please see my ring now?"

"Of course." Kerry helped her up and then opened her hand. Sasha plucked the ring from her palm, inspecting it in the light.

It was like nothing she'd ever seen before—a tapering spiral made from a dark, heavy material, its surface inlaid with small diamonds. A flash of green caught her gaze, and she realized that an emerald had been set into the broad end of the spiral.

"I made it." Kerry sounded nervous again, her words tumbling out in a rush. "From a nail I removed from this roof. It probably belongs in a museum, but everyone insisted I should keep it as a memento." She pointed to the interior of the ring. "First, I had to forge it into the spiral shape. It's inlaid with platinum here, where it will touch your finger. The emerald at the nail head is from a ring of my great-grandmother's, which she got in Ireland. It reminded me of your eyes. And the diamonds...well, they're forever. Which is what I want us to be."

For the second time in the past several minutes, Sasha couldn't believe her ears. "You made this? How? When?"

"There's a studio at Oxford. One of the Fine Arts students helped me. Every time we had to be apart because you had something official to do, I'd lock myself in there for hours." Kerry reached out to tuck a strand of hair behind Sasha's ear. "I wanted it to represent our relationship. Strong. Enduring. Precious."

"I love it." Sasha could barely speak through the emotion constricting her throat. "I love how it looks. I love that you created it and how much thought you put into its symbolism. I love you, Kerry."

"I love you, Sasha. So much." Kerry carefully took the ring between her fingers. "Hold out your hand." When she obeyed, Kerry positioned it at the very tip of her finger and then looked down into her eyes. "A princess belongs to her people. I know that will always be true. But I also want you to be mine."

She slid the ring into place, then bent to kiss it. When she withdrew, Sasha looked down at the sparkling diamonds, made all the more brilliant by the dark surface into which they'd been set. The ring fit perfectly. It felt so *right* on her hand, just as the presence of Kerry felt in her life.

"I am yours." She threaded her arms around Kerry's neck. "You're the only one who will ever know all of me. I will always belong to you in a way I belong to no one else."

The kiss was gentle but firm, like the promises they had just exchanged. It seemed to go on forever—Kerry's mouth moving over hers with tender purpose, Kerry's arms holding her close. When it finally ended, Sasha rested her cheek against Kerry's chest, listening to the rhythm of her heartbeat. One year ago, she wouldn't have been able to imagine this moment. Now she couldn't imagine a life without Kerry by her side.

"Shall we go back?" Kerry asked after several minutes had passed in silence. "You promised Lizzie, after all."

"I did." Sasha reluctantly took a step backward. "But just so you're prepared, at the first opportunity, I am dragging you off to bed."

"No dragging required." Kerry's eyes grew a shade darker. "I want to know what it's like to make love to my fiancée."

Sasha shivered at the note of intensity lacing her voice. "That sounds so good. Every word." Together, they descended the dais, but when they reached its foot, a sudden thought gave her pause. "I just have one favor to ask."

"Oh?"

"You're the most genuine person I've ever met. I love that about you. But tomorrow...can you pretend to be surprised?"

Kerry's burst of laughter echoed through Westminster Hall, filling its dark corners with sound. "I'll certainly do my best."

"That's all I can ask." She pulled Kerry forward. "Come on. Let's tell our family the good news."

GARGOYLE LOVERS

Sacchi Green

"I'm siingin' in the raaiin…" But that song was from the wrong Gene Kelly movie, and it wasn't quite raining and I was only whistling. My speaking voice gets me by, but singing blows the whole presentation.

Hal glanced down, her face stern in that exaggerated way that makes me tingle in just the right places. I shoved my hands into my pockets, skipped a step or two and knew she felt as good as I did. Hal's hardly the type to dance through the Paris streets like Gene Kelly, especially across square cobblestones, but there was a certain lilt to her gait.

Or maybe a swagger.

"That pretty-boy waiter was all over you," I said slyly. A gay guy making a pass always makes her day. "And giving me dirty looks every chance he got!"

"Lucky for you I'm not cruising for pretty boys, then. But don't give me too much lip or I might change my mind."

I couldn't quite manage penitence, but at least I knew better than to remind her that she already had a pretty boy, for better or worse. Still, some punishment games would be a fine end to the evening. Last night we'd been too jet-lagged to take proper advantage of the Parisian atmosphere. "That maître d' with a beak like a gargoyle was sure eyeing me, too, especially from behind." I gave another little skip.

Hal ignored the bait. "Thought you'd had your fill of gargoyles today." A cathedral wouldn't have been her first choice for honeymoon sightseeing, but the mini-balcony of our rental apartment had a stupendous view of Notre-Dame de Paris. I'd oohed and ahhed about gargoyles over our croissants and café au lait, so she'd humored me and we'd taken the tour.

To tell the truth, being humored by Hal unnerved me a bit. I didn't want being married to make a difference in our relationship. The fact that she'd shooed me out of that sex toy shop in Montmartre while she made a purchase was reassuring, but just in case, I decided I could manage some genuine penitence after all.

I hung my head and peered up at her slantwise. "I know I was a real pain. I can't figure out what it is about gargoyles that just gets to me. They're sort of scary, but not really, and sort of sad, and some of them are beautiful in a weird kind of way." Just as Hal was, but I'd never say so. "I'm sorry I went on about them like that."

"What makes you think they're sad? Just because their butts are trapped in stone?" She was trying to suppress a grin. I felt better.

"Well, I'd sure hate that, myself!"

That got me the squeeze on my ass I'd been angling for. "I'd rather have these sweet cheeks accessible," she said. The squeeze got harder than I'd bargained for, startling me into a grimace.

She eased off with a slow stroke between my thighs. "You should've seen your face just now. Could be there's something like that going on with the gargoyles. Not rage, or fear, or pain at all—unless it's pain so delicious it makes them howl with lust."

I was awestruck. Hal is generally the blunt, taciturn type, but I love it when her wicked imagination bursts forth. Almost as much as I love the vulnerability that once in a while gives an extra gruffness to her voice.

She was on a roll now, face alight like a gleeful demon. A lovable demon. "There's somebody hidden behind the stone, in another dimension, or time, or whatever, giving the gargoyle the fucking of its life. A reaming so fine it's been going on for centuries."

"Yes!" I was very nearly speechless. To lean out high above Paris, in the sun, wind and rain of eons, my face forever twisted in a paroxysm of fierce joy while Hal's thrusts filled me eternally with surging pleasure…

A few drops of rain began to fall, but that wasn't what made us hurry faster across the Pont de Saint-Louis. The great ornate iron gates at our apartment building had given me fantasies that morning of being chained, spread-eagled, against them, but now I rushed across the cobblestoned courtyard and through the carved oak door, so turned on that the four flights of stairs inside scarcely slowed me down—which might also have been because Hal's big hand on my butt was hurrying me along.

At our apartment, though, she held me back while she opened the door. "Over-the-threshold time. It'll be more official when we get back home, but this will have to do for now."

So I entered the room slung over Hal's shoulder, kicking a little for balance, until she dumped me amongst the red and gold brocade cushions on the couch. They went tumbling off as I struggled to get my pants lowered.

"Not here," she mused. "Maybe up there?" There was a sturdy railing across the loft that held the king-sized bed.

"Out there! Please?" The balcony was really only a space

where the French windows were set back into the wall about a foot, but there was an intricate iron fence along the edge, and with the windows wide open it had felt like balcony enough at breakfast time.

"Can you be quiet as a gargoyle?"

"You can gag me."

"No. I want to see your face." Hal pulled open the windows, grabbed the bag from the sex toy store, heaved me up and the next minute I was kneeling on the balcony and clutching the fence.

She moved aside a couple of pots of geraniums and tested the fence for strength and anchoring. "This would take even my weight," she muttered. In seconds she'd fastened my wrists to the railing with brand-new bonds that looked uncannily like chains of heavy iron links, even though they weren't hard as metal and had just a hint of stretch to them. "Feel enough like a gargoyle?"

"Mmm-hmm." I was drifting into a space I'd never known before. Lights from the Quai d'Anjou below and the quais across the Seine were reflected on the dark river, flickering like ancient torches as the water rippled past. Even the lights of modern Paris on the far bank took on a mellow glow that could have fit into any century.

"Hold that thought." Hal backed away into the room. I scarcely heard the rustling of the shop bag or the running of water in the bathroom. Then she was back, soundlessly, a dark looming presence that might have been made of stone.

The night air drew me into its realm. I leaned out over the railing as far as my bonds would allow, my butt raised high. Then Hal had one arm around my waist, holding me steady, while her other hand probed into my inner spaces that she knew so well. Need swelled inside me, shuddered through my body, catching in my throat as strangled, guttural groans. My face twisted with the struggle not to make too much noise, my mouth gaped open and my head flailed back and forth.

A whimper escaped when her hand withdrew, and so did a short, sharp bleat as something new replaced it; smooth, lubed, not quite familiar, not any of Hal's gear I'd felt before. I heard her heavy breathing, felt her thrusts and lost all sense of anything beyond the moment, anything beyond our bodies. A scream started forcing its way up through my chest and throat.

Just in time, Hal snapped open the bonds on my wrists, lifted me from behind and lurched with me across the plump back of the couch. With a rhythm accelerating like a Parisienne's motorbike she finished me off, then found her own slower, deep pace, and her own release. I could still barely breathe, but I managed to twist my neck enough to see her contorted face at that moment. Yes, magnificently beautiful in her own feral way.

In the aftermath we curled together, laughing when she showed me the new gargoyle-faced dildo slick with my juices. "Those French don't miss a trick when it comes to tourists," I said.

Hal grew quiet. I thought she was dozing, but after a while she cleared her throat. "Those French..." Her voice was unusually gruff. She tried again. "They claim to be tops in the lover department, too, I've heard. But I've got the best deal in the whole world with you. The best lover..." She stroked my still-simmering pussy. "The prettiest boy..." She touched my cheek. "The best wife...And the wildest gargoyle in all of France."

I remembered her face just minutes ago, and knew that the last part wasn't true. Still, the wisest response seemed to be a kiss that moved eventually from her mouth along her throat, and lower, and lower, with more daring than I'd ever risked before; and eventual proof that the best lover part, at least, was absolutely certain.

GOING TO THE CHAPEL

Giselle Renarde

When Deva and Yvonne burst into the church half an hour late for their own wedding, their knees were streaked with mud. Yvonne's gorgeous gown, the one she'd spent three months selecting, had grass stains all down the front. She'd paid more for that white dress than she'd paid for her first car, and look at it now—damaged beyond repair.

And Deva? Well, her retro turquoise suit hadn't fared much better. The left jacket sleeve was muddied from the cuff to the elbow, and don't even start about the pant legs!

They hadn't planned it—honestly, they hadn't—but when their families and friends all turned around to find them at the back of the church, surrounded by big bouquets of blue carnations, they both cried out, "It's not what you think!"

"You're not supposed to see the bride on the day of the wedding," Yvonne teased.

Deva raised a churlish brow. "Neither are you."

They locked gazes as mothers and aunts rushed around the

apartment. The brides constituted a still point in the chaos. They weren't giving in to their families' anxiety. Why get worked up about a wedding?

Taking one step closer, Deva grabbed Yvonne's hand. "Don't you wish we could ditch everyone and just...you know..."

Yvonne glanced toward the bed and bit her lip, trying not to smile too widely. "Get your mind out of the gutter. You'll shock your virgin bride."

"Ha!" Deva wrapped both arms around Yvonne and held her close, whispering into her ear. "I can't wait to get you home after the wedding."

"Mmm..."

Deva's hot breath warmed more than just Yvonne's ear, and she'd have given anything to surrender then and there, but her mother's voice rang out from the doorway. "Girls! It's time to get to get a move on. You don't want to be late for your own wedding."

Yvonne stepped away from Deva, covering the blush in her cheeks with both hands. "We're on our way."

Deva's mother appeared in the doorway behind Yvonne's and said, "I don't understand why you're walking. Who walks to church on her wedding day?"

"That's how we met." Deva leaned against the dresser while Yvonne sat on the bed. "Or, not how we *met,* but how we got to know each other."

"I only started going to that church because there was a rainbow flag on the sign," Yvonne said. "I've never been a churchy person, but it's hard to find a community when you move to a new place. I figured if they were queer-friendly it could be a start."

Her mother smiled. "Yes, I don't remember you wanting to go to church when you were little."

Yvonne shrugged. "Everyone's really nice at this one down the street. And it didn't hurt that there was a built, butch Indian chick sitting in the front pew every week—legs spread, an elbow on either knee, too cool for school. Kept me coming back for more."

"Deva!" said Yvonne's soon-to-be mother-in-law. "You shouldn't sit that way in church. Keep your knees together."

Deva bowed her head, obviously trying not to laugh. "Yes, Mother."

"We started walking home together when we realized we lived in the same apartment complex," Yvonne went on. "And soon she started picking me up and walking me to church, too."

"Yeah, and I just kept getting here earlier and earlier, until I was picking her up on Saturday night."

When Deva chuckled, her mother smacked her hip, aiming for her bottom. "Bad girl. You don't talk that way."

"Sure I do," Deva said, still laughing as her mother spanked her.

"If you weren't as big as your brothers, I would take you over my knee."

Yvonne and her mother cracked matching smiles as Deva and hers teased one another. And then Yvonne's high-strung mom looked at her watch and said, "We really should leave for the church. It's getting to be that time. Don't want your guests thinking you've come down with a case of cold feet."

"You guys head out," Deva said, shuffling her mom and Yvonne's toward the front door. "We're gonna stroll hand in hand, just like we did when we first started walking together."

"Aww," said one of Deva's aunts, who'd been hiding out in the living room. "There's nothing like young love."

Yvonne laughed. "We're not exactly *young*."

"Well, you were when you met," the aunt said. "How long ago was that? Five years?"

"Almost," Deva said, then winked at Yvonne. "Feels like yesterday."

Yvonne nodded. "I know what you mean."

It was like the honeymoon period never ended. They were still loopy in love, and so sizzling hot for each other they couldn't keep their hands to themselves. Hopefully the wedding wouldn't change all that. But why would it? A marriage is only a commitment, and they were already committed to each other.

Nevertheless, as their mothers and aunts filtered out the door, a feeling of apprehension came over Yvonne. This was it. Today was the day. No going back.

"What's wrong?" Deva asked when everyone else was gone.

"Hmm?" She plastered on a smile. "Nothing. I'm fine. How 'bout you?"

Deva cocked her head, not buying it. "Okay…"

There was something about Deva, like she could look into Yvonne's eyes and see right straight through to her soul. Made her nervous and fidgety as hell. She walked to the window, waiting to see their family members filter out the lobby door.

Deva took her from behind, wrapping both arms around her waist. "Tell me what you're thinking, babe."

Yvonne pressed her forehead to the window. "Nothing. Just…are you ready for this?"

"For what?"

She laughed. "Marriage. Me."

Deva hugged her harder. "We already live together. If I couldn't stand you, I think I'd know it by now."

"I guess so…"

"Why?" Deva asked. "Are you having second thoughts?"

Yvonne watched her mother and Deva's and all their aunts spill from the front door like an ocean wave. "No," she said, decidedly. "I want to marry you."

She turned around, and Deva kissed her, softly, on the lips. "I want to marry you, too."

Why did that embarrass her so much? She felt an inexplicable blush coming on as she slipped away from the window, away from Deva. "My mom was right. We should get a move on or people will wonder."

"I'm starting to wonder…"

"Wonder what?"

Deva shook her head. "Nothing."

Yvonne grabbed her phone off the coffee table and shoved it down the side of her wedding dress.

Deva cracked up. "What are you doing?"

With a shrug, Yvonne said, "I'm not bringing a purse and you never know when you might need a phone. In case of emergencies. You know?"

This time, Deva shrugged. "I'm not bringing mine."

"But you've got the house keys?"

Deva plucked them out of her pocket. "Sure you don't want a quickie before we head to the chapel?"

"When have I ever wanted a quickie?" Yvonne laughed as she opened the door. "I want you all…night…long."

When Deva raced at her, she leapt into the hall like a matador teasing a bull. They locked up and rode the elevator down to the ground floor. Their neighbors would think they were crazy—not that they actually knew many people in the neighborhood, aside from fellow churchgoers.

And Mr. Rosetti.

Yvonne groaned as they stepped into the lobby.

"What's wrong?" Deva took her hand and squeezed it. "I'm worried about you."

"No, it's nothing. I just hope Mr. Rosetti isn't out gardening when we walk by. He's the last person I need to deal with today."

Deva let out a sympathetic sigh. "Well, we'll just ignore him if he is. What's the worst he can do?"

"Recite scripture at us." The automated lobby doors opened for them and they walked through, greeted by the gorgeous summer sun. "I'm so sick of people like him. Why can't they just mind their own business? They act like every queer person in the world somehow threatens their sense of...I don't even know what!"

Deva escorted her to the sidewalk. "Don't get so worked up about it. Today's your wedding day—nothing can spoil it."

"Unless you run out on me."

Deva laughed. "Well, you don't have to worry about that."

As they crossed the tree-lined street, sun dappled their finery and their flesh. Yvonne soaked up the warmth like a dozing kitten, at once calm and exhilarated by the prospect of saying "I do" in front of all their friends and family.

But once they'd set foot on the shady side of the street, apprehension snuck into her heart. She remembered the first time Deva had scooped up her hand and held it, the first time they'd walked home from church like that, together, as a unit. Yvonne remembered it so clearly because of the man in 129.

He'd eyed them from the garden as they walked by his house—those beady, dark eyes fixed on their fingers as they chatted and flirted. Yvonne still remembered how giddy she'd felt as she set her head on Deva's shoulder for the first time, when suddenly a rumbling voice cut through their bliss.

"You! You gays—why don't you stay downtown with the rest of the sinners? The suburbs are for good, god-fearing people. You're the reason I had to find another church!"

Yvonne had whipped around to face him, too stunned to speak. Deva only said, "What?"

"That church at the end of the street—I went there from the time I moved into this house in 1973. And then you gays convince that woman minister to perform your sinful ceremonies and forced me out."

"Sinful ceremonies?" Deva asked. "What ceremonies?"

"Gay marriage!" Mr. Rosetti threw his hands in the air, over-emphasizing the simple words.

Yvonne laughed, even though she was shocked and taken aback. She laughed because she'd been picturing this "sinful" gay ceremony as some orgiastic devil worship. But marriage? He was walking about marriage?

"You think gay marriage is sinful?" Deva asked.

His eyes bugged out. "It goes against god!"

"How?" Deva's chest puffed a bit, the way it always did when she got into a battle of words. "How can love possibly go against god? God is love."

"Hippies," he spat. "Hippie queers, drive me from my church—*my* church. Not yours."

"Come on, Deva. Let's just go." Yvonne had yanked her by the arm, pulled her down the sidewalk as she railed against the homophobe at 129.

The first hurt felt just as fresh as every other insult he'd heaped on since. As they approached his house en route to their wedding, Yvonne's heart clenched. *Please, god, don't let him be outside.*

And he wasn't.

Praise the Lord.

Wait a second...what was that? As they approached Mr. Rosetti's garden, a shape in the dirt caught Yvonne's eye. It started on the lawn and then stretched out across the marigolds. Oh no...it wasn't, was it? Yes, it was. A body!

She tightened her grip on Deva's hand, but Deva was two steps ahead, climbing up the rock garden and over the slight incline between the sidewalk and the lawn. "Mr. Rosetti? Are you okay?"

When Deva fell to her knees, Yvonne shrieked. "You're gonna get your tux all dirty!"

Like Deva cared about clothes. "Come on, get up here. Help me roll him over."

"Is he...dead?" Yvonne whispered the word, like she'd be inviting the Grim Reaper if she said it too loudly.

"I don't know. I don't think so. Would you just get up here and give me a hand?"

Yvonne inched two steps up the driveway without taking her eyes off Mr. Rosetti's prone body. "But if he *is* dead, there's no point getting all dirty trying to revive him."

Deva's eyes blazed. "Would you stop acting like a child, Yvonne? You're a grown woman. Time to behave that way."

By interrupting her wedding day to work on a homophobic corpse? What was the point? If Mr. Rosetti hated gay people so much, he probably wouldn't want a pair of lesbians putting their hands all over him anyway.

But Yvonne could only hold out so long before her better judgment kicked in. She stepped from the driveway onto the lawn and her heels slumped into the soft ground. When she took another step, the shoes remained wedged in the dirt. "Damn it."

"Help me roll him," Deva said, her voice firm and commanding.

"How?" Yvonne didn't want to touch the guy, but she also didn't want to admit that to Deva.

"Just help his head along while I turn his body, okay?"

"Okay." Yvonne wasn't going to argue at this stage. She held her hands near his hair, but couldn't bring herself to touch him—not until Deva heaved his shoulder. Then Yvonne worried that if she didn't do anything, the old man's neck might snap when Deva rolled him over.

"Good job," Deva said, though Yvonne didn't feel like she was doing anything.

She closed her eyes as her hands found his head. Somehow, when Deva turned him, he ended up with his head on her thigh. She screamed when she looked down to find his face covered in dirt.

"Brush that off," Deva said.

"He's dead! He's dead!" Yvonne tried to escape, only to discover Deva had rolled the man onto her bulky wedding dress. "Dev, I'm stuck."

"It's okay, babe." Deva grabbed the lace train of her veil and used it to brush soil from the old man's skin.

"What are you doing?" Yvonne shrieked.

"In case we need to do CPR."

Yvonne's throat squeaked. "I'm not putting my mouth on his mouth."

"I don't think you'll have to." Deva place a hand on his chest and remained quiet for a moment. "He's breathing."

"Oh, thank god."

"Mr. Rosetti?" Deva tapped his cheek, then smacked it. "Mr. Rosetti, can you hear me?"

"What's wrong with him?" Yvonne asked.

"I don't know. Get out your phone."

"What for?"

"To call 911."

"Oh." Yvonne wanted to put up some argument, but she couldn't think of any reason why she shouldn't call—well, aside from the fact that they were late for their own wedding. She reached into her restrictive wedding gown and pulled out her phone. Her fingers fumbled as she punched in the number and waited for something to happen.

A woman's voice came on the line and asked, "What is the nature of your emergency?"

Yvonne looked to Deva. "What do I say?"

"You know what to say," Deva told her.

"What is the nature of your emergency?"

"Our neighbor…we found him on the lawn. He's not…well, he's breathing, but he won't wake up."

"He's unconscious?"

"I don't know. I'm not a doctor."

"Is he awake?" the operator asked.

"No."

"Does he smell like he's been drinking?"

Yvonne sniffed him. "No, he smells like plants. He was working in the garden, looks like."

The 911 operator asked where to send the ambulance and Yvette gave her Mr. Rosetti's address. The operator then rolled out instructions that fell out of her brain the moment she'd repeated them to Deva. *Do this, do that. Check this, check that.* And then something stuck: "Reach into his mouth and make sure his tongue isn't blocking his airway."

Deva looked up at the phone, eyes wide as saucers.

Yvonne shrugged.

Neither of them did anything. Where were finger cots when you needed them?

He was breathing. His chest rose and fell. They didn't really need to put their fingers in his mouth, did they?

"Have you done it yet?" the operator asked.

"My wife is doing it," Yvonne said. "Or, not my wife—not yet. My fiancée. We were on our way to our wedding when we found him."

"Oh," the operator replied, hesitantly, like she wasn't entirely sure how to respond. "Well, congratulations. The ambulance should be arriving in a matter of minutes."

"He's a terrible person," Yvonne said. "He hates us. He hates lesbians, hates gay people. He thinks we go against god. And look at this! It's our wedding day and instead of standing up in church, we're shoving our fingers in his mouth."

"Well, not really," Deva whispered.

"You're very likely saving his life," the 911 operator said. "You're doing a good thing."

Yvonne's eyes filled unexpectedly with tears. She choked them back. She didn't want to cry on her wedding day, not for any reason.

"Now," the operator went on, "if your neighbor starts vomiting you'll need to dig into his throat and pull out any traces of stomach contents so he doesn't choke. Are you prepared to do that?"

Deva obviously heard what the operator had asked, because her jaw dropped. For a moment, she just stared at Yvonne, stared at the phone. Deva was the strong one, the ready-for-anything partner, but would she go so far as to dig vomit from a homophobe's throat?

"Sure," Yvonne said. "Why not?"

Deva burst out in silent laughter, chuckling so hard her shoulders shook.

Yvonne egged her on. "Of course we'll remove Mr. Rosetti's regurgitated stomach contents on our wedding day. We's good people, over here."

Deva fell to the side, rolling on Mr. Rosetti's lawn and laughing her ass off. Nothing spelled joy like Deva's laughter. It made Yvonne smile so hard her jaw hurt.

The 911 operator didn't seem quite so amused. "Is the patient breathing?"

Yvonne watched his chest rise and fall. "Yup."

"And still unconscious?"

This time, Yvonne shouted his name. When he didn't react,

she slapped him in the face. Still nothing, but *damn* that felt good. "He's out like a light."

"The ambulance is on its way. I'll need you to stay with him until the paramedics arrive."

"Sure." Yvonne cast her gaze in Deva's direction. Something behind her had caught her wife-to-be's attention. She turned to find a woman with a dog, a man holding a small child on her bicycle, and a group of joggers grouped around the sidewalk, their attentive gazes fixed on the scene like they were watching live-action reality TV.

Yvonne didn't know how to feel—like the star of the show? Or was that Deva's role?

"What happened?" one of the joggers asked, breaking the fourth wall.

Deva responded. "We don't know. We found him passed out in the garden. He's breathing, but we can't wake him up."

"You should have left him there," said the woman with the dog. "That guy's a jerk. He deserves to die."

When she walked off, Yvonne exchanged knowing glances with Deva. In that woman's place, Yvonne probably would have said the same thing. She still wasn't sure why she felt good about helping someone who'd never been anything but nasty to her. Maybe it was just the right thing to do—help him because he was human and he was in trouble.

"I hear voices," the 911 operator said. "Has the patient regained consciousness?"

"No, it's just people from the neighborhood. They don't like this guy any more than we do."

The operator sounded like she was about to say something, but then fell silent.

Deva looked up, over the assembled crowd, as sirens rang out from the main street, approaching fast.

"The ambulance?" Yvonne asked.

Deva nodded and signaled to the crowd to get out of the way. The man and child moved a smidge, but the joggers remained exactly where they were, like they just had to find out how the show would end.

The ambulance roared onto the street, tearing toward the crowd. Yvonne could just see it knocking all those joggers over like bowling pins. Then they'd end up with two emergency situations to deal with.

The joggers shifted as a pair of paramedics spilled out of the vehicle. They raced up the driveway, and then onto the lawn. A black man and an Asian woman, both in bulky blue uniforms, lifted Mr. Rosetti off Yvonne's grass-stained wedding gown.

"We'll take over from here," the woman said, shooing Yvonne and Deva away.

Yvonne had grown so accustomed to the weight of Mr. Rosetti's head on her thigh that it felt weird to be without it. "We found him unconscious on the lawn, here. He's breathing, but we couldn't wake him up."

"We'll take over," the man repeated, driving the point home.

Deva helped Yvonne to her feet, and they inched down the rock garden together. "Wait, my shoes."

One of the paramedics was half sitting on them, and it took Deva's daring to sneak dangerously close to her butt and pluck them out of the earth.

"I thought they'd want us to help or something," Yvonne said. "Or I thought they'd at least ask us for information."

"I guess they got it from dispatch," Deva replied.

Yvonne looked down at the phone in her hand, and then brought it to her ear. "The ambulance is here. The paramedics have taken over."

The operator offered a word of thanks, but that was that. Why hadn't she wished them a happy wedding day before hanging up? Maybe she had to stick to a script or maybe she'd forgotten already, but it would have been nice.

Another paramedic came out of nowhere, clearing the sidewalk by asking the crowd to give them space. Yvonne let Deva drag her away, but she said, "I want to know what's happening. I want to know what's wrong with him."

"Me too, but we've got a wedding to get to, in case you've forgotten."

Yvonne smiled as one of the joggers asked, "Are you two getting married?"

Well, duh! Why else would they be dressed in a bridal gown and a tux?

Deva said, "Yeah, we're getting married right now, right down the street. Want to come?"

Yvonne laughed, but Deva was serious.

"No, that's okay," the jogger said. "We don't want to impose."

"You're not imposing. We're inviting you." Deva looked from the group of joggers to the man with the bicycle girl. "Everybody loves a wedding. And we're all neighbors. Might as well."

The dad looked to his little girl and shrugged. "Want to watch the heroes get married?"

Heroes. Yvonne's heart swelled.

The little girl chewed her hair and bashfully nodded. She whispered to her father, "They're all dirty."

"That's because they just saved a man's life."

One of the joggers said, "If they're coming to the wedding, I wouldn't mind going."

"Me too," another one said.

"Yeah, I love weddings."

Yvonne looked to Deva. "Should we go home and change first?"

"We're late enough as it is." Deva gave her an obvious once over—her dress was a disaster, but so was Deva's tux. "And think about it. We'll always have a story to tell."

"True." Yvonne dusted a bit of dirt from her sullied white dress. "Better get a move on, I guess."

So, hand in hand, they took off down the sidewalk, followed by a train of joggers and a girl on a bicycle kicking up the rear. Yvonne would like to say she never looked back, but that wasn't entirely true. She did look—to see if the paramedics were carrying Mr. Rosetti into the ambulance. As much as she despised the guy, she couldn't help wondering what happened to him, why he'd lost consciousness. Maybe he'd seen the lesbian brides marching up the sidewalk and fainted dead away.

They'd probably find out through the grapevine at some point in the future. Anyway, they'd devoted enough of their wedding day to him. The rest of the day was all theirs.

Squeezing her bride-to-be's hand, Yvonne said, "I love you, Dev."

"I love you, too."

Deva leaned in and gave her a sweet kiss. As they walked in the sunlight, the crowd behind them cheered. *Going to the chapel, and we're grungy and grass-stained...*

FOREVER YOURS, EILEEN

Rebekah Weatherspoon

I'm sitting in a Manhattan diner with my grandson June. He's named after me and right now he's driving me nuts. I would have come alone, but I'm waiting for Eileen. It's been fifteen years since we've seen each other, so yes, I'm nervous. Juney offered to be my support today. I wanted to turn him down, but his chatter is distracting me. He came out to me when he was very young. We helped each other, I like to think. He's the right person to have by my side.

He reaches across the table toward the stack of envelopes I've tucked under my arm. I smack his fingers away.

"Ow, Grandma!" He laughs, though.

"You know better than to get all grabby."

"I can't believe you save all of these letters."

It was Mama's idea initially. Keep all the letters, and one day when we're old ladies, we can laugh about them. I'm too anxious to laugh now.

I shrug and gaze out the diner window. I think about the

pages and pages I have in my hands, and there's not a second thought about having a choice in the matter. God wanted me to keep the letters. The letters are what got us here.

"Can I please read one?" June asks.

"Fine, but don't rip it." I reach down to the bottom and pull out the first envelope. There's two letters tucked inside, the first letter I ever wrote to Eileen, and the first letter she ever wrote back.

It's April 1956, and we're driving away from our home. Mama and Daddy fought for weeks over selling the farm. It was the first piece of anything Granddaddy ever owned. Mama was born in that house, but as Daddy has said a whole heap of times, "The South ain't what it should be, and it's time for us to go." Mama's upset because Grandma won't come with us. She's too old for the Klan to bother her, she says. She moves in with our uncle, who says he's not scared enough to walk away from his job in Jackson. Daddy calls him a fool, but he understands. My uncle doesn't have any sons.

I'm only nine, and even though I understand why we're leaving, I cry all the way to Tennessee. Later, after I have three sons of my own I'm finally able to wrap my mind around my parents' decision. You do what you have to do for your children. Daddy can fight for himself, but he doesn't trust his boys in the hands of Jim Crow. All the same, I cry with my head on Fredrick's shoulder all the way across the state line. I already miss Grandma and our dog Mickey. Mr. Hammond bought him with the farm because he's good at chasing small creatures that like to tear up the garden. Most of all, I miss Eileen.

She's my best friend in the world. We met when we were knee-high in Sunday school, and our mamas would joke that it would take the hand of god to pull us little devils apart.

The hand of god or my daddy's determination. Mama said I could write Eileen letters. It would be a great way for me to work on my spelling and my penmanship. Plus I'd have my very own pen pal. And that's what I did. The minute we got to Brooklyn I wrote Eileen a letter, not caring a lick about my penmanship.

> *Dear Eileen, I hate it here. The people are weird. There's no grass and everything smells like gasoline and poop.*

My grandson looks up from the paper. He's about to crumple with laughter. "Brooklyn smelled like poop in the fifties?"

"When you're used to fresh air everything in the city smells like poop. Do you want to read the letter or do you want to make fun of me?"

He laughs again. "Sorry. I'll be good."

It takes forever for me to hear back from Eileen, but her first letter is the first bright spot in our move. We come all this way and Fredrick gets beat up on his first day of school. George gets mussed up trying to help him. It takes Daddy forever to find work. Almost four months go by with the five of us living in my cousin's living room. Mama is cleaning rooms at this lousy hotel. She's exhausted every time she comes home, but she's always looking on the bright side. We finally get our own place, and the last day I'm helping Mama pack up our things, the mailman brings Eileen's letter.

> *Dear Juney, Sorry it took me so long to write back. I was waiting for something juicy to happen so I'd have some news. Nothing happened. Mama said you all were smart to leave. I asked her if we could move*

to Brooklyn too even though you said it was bad, but she said no.

"I can't handle how adorable this letter is," my grandson says.

I shrug again. "We were adorable kids."

"Are you nervous?"

"No."

"Well, you look fly, Grandma."

I glance down at my leather jacket and my matching boots. June helped picked out my jeans. He keeps me young. Finally I smile. "Thanks, baby."

"Let me read one more." I fish out the last letter I sent in junior high school. After that Eileen and I both start to mature, and there's things your grandchild doesn't need to know.

I write to her about Mrs. Stein and how she's invited me to take her ballet classes. Mama is wary at first, but after Mrs. Stein explains that her dream of dancing again is what got her through the war, Mama knows I'm in good hands. I hear people aren't so happy about her teaching mixed classes, but no one tries to stop her. I tell Eileen everything I'm learning, all the French terms. I promise I'll show her if we get to see each other again. When she writes back, she promises we will.

She writes me about the etiquette classes they started offering at the church and how her mama is making her go after she caught Eileen wiping her hands on the back of her sister's dress.

Our junior year in high school, Eileen writes me about her first boyfriend. Mama won't let me date. Some of my friends at school have steadies, but I think they are all jokers and my friends are silly for mooning over them. I want to think that maybe Eileen will shed some light on the appeal of liking a boy, but as I read her letter I find something other than curiosity rising in my mind.

It's a strange thing, Juney. I thought it would be different. Clara Winston and her boyfriend are always pawing at each other, but Harry doesn't want to neck or anything. He's going to college in the fall and he wants to be a doctor. I asked why he's not trying to get in my pants, and he said a gentleman waits until he's married. How sweet is that? I think that's why I like him. He's smart and he's going places and he listens to me when I talk. It's not a game of grabby hands when we're together. We did kiss, though. It was nice.

She sounds happy in the letter, and I'm happy for her, but later when I reread those particular pages I realize how jealous I was. I wait a while before I write back. I tell Mama about Eileen's boyfriend. She assures me it won't last. "It's just young love, Juney. He'll move on when he goes off to school."

"But you and Daddy met when you were young," I remind her.

"And I was the only girl around who wasn't bucktoothed or his cousin." She's teasing to make me feel better. When I finally answer Eileen's letter, I ask an obnoxious number of questions about Harry. When she writes back she tells me she's sorry for talking about him so much. I think she means it.

After a time, I finally see Eileen again. I've finished my third year at SUNY and she's finished her third year at Spelman. The government's just sent Fredrick's body back to us from Vietnam. Mama's a mess and she makes George promise he'll dodge if his number comes up. Daddy doesn't argue. I do what I can to hold it together, but I fall apart when I call Eileen. I can't wait for her reply in a letter. She lets me sob in her ear for as long as Daddy will let me be on the phone.

I come unhinged again when she shows up with her daddy at

the funeral. She holds my hand the whole time, and I think that's the moment I realize I love her. I can't put it into words yet, but the warmth of her fingers is the first real comfort I've felt since we left Mississippi. I don't want her to leave, but of course she does. Her daddy can only miss so much work.

The following Christmas, Harry proposes to her. She calls me. I convince her that I'm happy for them. We all go down for the wedding that spring. Fredrick's with us too because a year later the war is still going strong and the cloud of his death hasn't lifted. Eileen looks beautiful. I can't keep my eyes off her, and I let the joy of seeing her and the comfort of being home get me through the day. I'm cordial to Harry, genuinely grateful that he does seem like a nice man. On the trip back to New York, I cry again. I tell Mama I miss Fred.

Back in Brooklyn I quickly find that I make a good secretary, but I make an even better dancer. I ask Mrs. Rosenbaum, Mrs. Stein's daughter, if she'll let me teach a class at her studio. She says yes. I meet Walter on the bus one night on my way back from class. He's new to the city from Boston. He likes that I still have traces of my accent. He walks me all the way home one night and many more nights after. He asks Daddy if he can marry me. I beg Daddy to say yes, not because I love Walter, but because I know I'm supposed to. Daddy says yes.

I call Eileen to tell her the news. She tells me she's pregnant. I think we both pretend to be happy for each other. We keep writing to each other. I actually find that her pregnancy mends things I didn't realize were broken. She focuses on the baby now and not Harry or her church friends. I like hearing about her joys and her fears of being a mother. She's too far along to come to our wedding, but I send her a few pictures and she sends us pictures of her baby girl.

After that, our kids are all we talk about.

* * *

It's not a particular movement on the street that catches my eye, it's Eileen. I'd see her anywhere. At any distance, in any crowd. She passes by the window, her daughter and two grandkids in tow. The bell rings on the diner door and I spring to my feet. The introductions are a blur except for the one moment Sandra looks at me. She hates me. Eileen's told me in her letters that she's taken the news the hardest. You'd think it was me that killed her father and not the heart attack.

Even though her upbringing keeps her from saying so, she wishes her mother were anywhere but in this diner with me. It's written all over her face. Still she smiles at June and half smiles at me. I smile back and keep from laying out the truth she doesn't want to hear. I've waited nearly fifty years to be with her mother again. Her attitude is not going to keep us apart.

"Mom, are you settled?" Sandra finally says.

Eileen looks at me with an anxious smile. "Yeah. You kids go on. I'll see you back at the hotel."

Sandra says okay before she turns to June. "We have an extra ticket to *The Lion King*—"

"Just in case these two chickened out?"

I call on all of Jesus to keep from smacking the boy in the back of the head.

Sandra and her kids all chuckle at his joke. "Yes. Would you like to come along?"

"Sure. I know some people. Maybe I can get you backstage." With that June sweeps them out the door with his charm. Sandra glances back one more time before they disappear down the street.

Eileen and I are still standing in the aisle, just looking at each other. We sit, suddenly nervous again when a waitress comes bustling by. It's been a long time. We're both older. We're both grayer, but nothing about either of us has changed.

"You look great, Juney," she finally says.

"So do you."

I ask her about her trip. She confesses that Sandra is still worried. Then she asks to see the letters. There are so many things I want to do. Making love to her being at the top of the list, but I need to give her time. I slide the stack across the table and then I wait. Our coffee comes, and then her salad. I order some fries and pie, and I watch her as she reads.

I had a feeling which letter she was looking for. I've read it over a hundred times, when I was preparing to leave Walter and on so many nights after I found myself alone in a tiny apartment, wishing I had the money to take my youngest baby with me.

It's the letter I wrote before I convinced Walter that we needed a vacation. I told him I wanted the boys to see their Southern roots. I promised him some romance near the swimming hole if it was still there. Really I want to see Eileen. She and Harry are more than happy to have us. Once we arrive and the boys are settled in chasing Eileen's girls all over her yard, and Harry's convinced Walter to play some dominos, Eileen and I set off down her road on our own.

We walk for a while. She tells me about her girls driving her crazy. I tell her about the fast hussies sniffing around my boys now that they've shot up. She gets quiet, though, after a while and then she says, "I was thinking about what you said in your letter about Walter, about it not being him."

"About men in general?"

"Yeah. I think about that sometimes too." We stop walking. I hear crickets everywhere, even the warm air moving around us as I turn to look at Eileen. She looks at the ground.

"I don't...I don't think I have those feelings for Harry anymore."

I hear the words, but they don't make sense. I wrote that letter because I had to put those emotions somewhere before I burst. I think all women have a sense of wanting more or something different. It's in our blood, I think, but we deal with what we're dealt. I expect her to understand a little bit about feeling somewhat trapped or looking at a man after fifteen years and wondering if you can stomach fifteen more because you don't know when you'll ever get a chance to live for yourself. But that part I wrote and didn't take back about men in general? I didn't expect Eileen to understand that.

I try to play it off. "Maybe you just need to get the spark back." I say that foolish thing knowing how phony it sounds. I'm glad she doesn't give up.

"That's not what I mean, Juney. I don't think I feel that way about Harry anymore. Or anyone really. 'Cept you."

Her eyes meet mine. She's open and vulnerable, and I don't know what I'm thinking because we're out in the middle of the road, but I kiss her. The strangest part is not that I'm kissing my best friend, but that she doesn't seem shocked. She's kissing me back, guiding us sightless off the road until my back touches the rough bark of a tall pine. The scratching sensation through my shirt brings me back down to earth and I realize this kiss is real, not something I've made up in my mind. I know now that I've been kissing the wrong lips all along.

We break apart and I see that Eileen is just as scared as I am. She takes a step back and touches her lips. But that fear isn't disgust or shame. It's a realization. It's the truth.

"How do we do this?" I ask, because I know now for sure it's not Walter who I want to be with. It's not men at all.

"I don't think we can."

My heart sinks, but I understand how she feels. It's more than this feeling between us. It's our babies. It's these two men who've given us everything. Walter who's worked so we can afford for me to teach dance for next to nothing, and Harry who allows Eileen to stay home with the girls. It's friends and family. For Eileen it's church and community. How do we turn our backs on that?

I grab her and kiss her again. It's a final kiss. At least it is for a time. I know this is not our fairy-tale ending, that we won't get to experience that life, but I kiss her so she knows without a doubt how I feel. When I'm hundreds of miles away it's her I'll be thinking about. I kiss her again so I can remember how kissing is supposed to feel in your toes, in your gut. I want to remember the fireworks her lips set off between my legs. She moans and I know she feels it too. A truck rumbles on the gravel a ways down the road and we jump apart. It's just a neighbor, Eileen explains as the man drives by. He waves and we wave back and then we head back toward home.

It's a long time before I write Eileen again. I didn't know what to say. That kiss broke something in me, for better or for worse. I can't look at Walter the same. Every intimate moment we have, it's thoughts of Eileen that help me finish. Everything in my life is a lie.

Her next letter is the one that changes everything. The paper is nearly falling apart, I've read it so many times. It's short, but it says everything I need to hear.

> *Dear Juney, I love you. I'm putting on a brave face for Harry and the kids, but I'm thinking of you all the time. I can't leave him. He's innocent in all this, and it feels wrong to just toss him aside because of feelings I can't control, and I have to think about the kids too, but I do love you. My heart is yours, Eileen*

Eileen looks up from the pages.

"I wrote this while Cole was napping. Woke her up and we went right to the post office."

"This was the one you didn't want Harry to find," I say. In her next letter she begged me to burn it. I didn't.

"I didn't want Harry to find any of them. I'm glad you kept it."

After that we barely mention our husbands and our kids anymore. We talk about what we want, what we wish we had. I tell her, now that I'm paying closer attention, I know women who are living together. People think them widowed or sisters or even just strange, but they are making it work. Eileen understands, but she can't leave Harry. Still she writes. The letters become more frequent and more open. I keep them all.

Dear Juney, I had a dream about you last night. You were chasing me through the pines. The sun was out and it was raining. I let you catch me this time. Even though we can't be together, you are still in my heart. Forever yours, Eileen

We go five more years without seeing each other. Between her letters, I focus on the boys and my students. Slowly, I start to let Walter go. It starts with my classes, more students now that the boys are older. More Saturday afternoons apart and more evenings where I leave dinner for him in the fridge. Then I start coming to bed later and later. It's easier to deny a man who's already asleep. He asks me once if there's someone else. I don't even sound offended when I tell him no.

Later that week I meet a woman at the library. There's no attraction, but she tells me about a great dance workshop they're having at NYU. I hide my left hand the whole time and don't tell her I'm married. When I meet her by the ticket booth a few days later, my ring is zipped into my purse. I tell Eileen about her in my next letter. I'm happy to hear that she's jealous when she writes back.

There's a spring wedding. Eileen's oldest, Patricia, is pregnant, but that's between the families and the pages of our letters. Eileen invites us down. Walter agrees, thinking we'll find our romance somewhere in that Southern heat, but all I find is Eileen the morning of the ceremony. We're alone in the powder room at the church. She doesn't say a word, but her eyes tell me everything. She's been waiting for this one stolen moment for us. I seize it, not knowing if we'll ever get another. I kiss her, and this time it's aching and pain and relief. We've had time apart, time to think things through, but the feelings haven't changed. I love her and I know she loves me too.

"I don't know what to do," she whispers as my lips brush her forehead. I know what I want her to do, but mostly it's what I want for myself. I don't have it in me to ask Eileen to be that selfish.

"We endure it."

She stares back at me and I offer her what I can of a reassuring smile. She nods. I hold her a moment longer even though I know we are out of time. We both turn back to the mirror and fix our lipstick. The last time I dance with Walter is at that reception.

Six months later I move out. I tell Walter 90 percent of the truth: that I'm gay and that I can't be with him anymore. He doesn't understand, and neither do the boys. I'm the villain for a long time, but I know the decision is right. My confidence wavers, though, when I see that I've made this decision alone. I'm free of Walter, but no closer to Eileen. It's a struggle not to beg in my letters to her. It takes everything I have to balance an expression of love and the bottomless desperation that claws at my heels.

Harry's heart attack surprises everyone, but I'm relieved by Eileen's first letter after his funeral. I don't think it's appropriate for me to attend.

> Dear Juney, I don't know how to say this, but I will. I miss Harry. He was a good man. I already miss his companionship and I miss him for the kids, but I feel free. Is that horrible for me to say? I know it is, but I've always told you the truth. How much longer can you wait for me? Forever Yours, Eileen.

By now there are cell phones and we text each other pictures of our grandkids, but I need my reply documented correctly.

Forever, I write back.

It doesn't take forever, but it feels that way. Four more years. Two for the kids. A year for them to process that she is not what they thought her to be. And in that time, months to learn of her feelings for me, time for them to form an opinion on those feelings. Eileen's pre-diabetic and her doctor wants her to lose a few pounds. She says she wants to look good for me. There's another year, and then Eileen needs some time for herself. I tell her I can wait. She calls me late one night.

"We should take a trip first. I want to go to Las Vegas and Paris. You can show me all the fancy French you learned."

I think of the money Walter was kind enough to tell me to save, and Eileen tells me she has plenty from Harry.

"We'll take a trip, then." I feel myself smiling in the dark. "What do we do after the trip?"

"I figure if I can handle traveling with you, I can handle living with you."

"You want to move to New York?"

"You keep saying the city keeps you young."

"That's true, but—"

"Then I'll come live with you. After our trip. Night." She hangs up before I can argue. Later, though, I give her a practical out. If the trip is too overwhelming, she can go back to Mississippi with no fight from me. With all this time gone by, I need her to be happy.

She's near now and I can't read the expression on her face.

"Will you touch me?" she asks. I get up and scoot into the booth beside her. Under the table I take her hand. Everything feels right. For a moment.

"I thought it would be easier. I thought I would feel…lighter. Freer?" she says.

"But you don't."

"I don't know how you made it through. I never thought I could be so lonely."

I hold my breath and think things through before I react. She's sad. She's hurting, but she's here. That matters.

"What do we do?"

"We travel. Like we planned," she says.

"I want you to be sure."

"I am."

"Then we'll decide when we get back."

"I said, I am." She shakes her head and tries again. "I'm saying this all wrong. I think I feel guilty. About Harry and the kids. I feel bad because I feel so good about being here with you. I've wanted to be here with you all along."

"You know what I've realized," I say. "It's okay to feel two ways about things. It's okay that you care about your family and their needs. I never wanted that to stop."

"I know."

I turn and look at Eileen. For once it's not a secret. We don't have to hide. I kiss her. She kisses me back. We keep it tame because we're in public and there's no need to frighten the young people. Later, things will get more interesting.

She sighs and puts her head on my shoulder. We're nine again, hiding under the church porch. Eileen yawns and tells me her grandma lost another tooth. I laugh to myself and tell Eileen why. She laughs too and squeezes my hand back.

I kiss her again, and this time we have an audience.

"Ow, ow! Get it, Grandma." Two teenagers at the counter are watching us. The yeller winks. Her friend gives us a thumbs-up and a toothy grin. Beside me, Eileen laughs and I feel it down in my gut. She's happy. She's relieved. And so am I.

BEAUTIFUL

Teresa Noelle Roberts

As Alexis led Jane to the chain web in the center of the still-empty dungeon and told her what she planned for the first play party since the surgery, Jane's heart threatened to burst through her scarred chest. It took all her courage not to safeword or simply start a plain vanilla argument with her girlfriend and domme.

She used to love being on display, an object to be enjoyed by the eyes and roving hands of the other party guests. Loved the eyes on her. Loved Alexis's pride as people admired her sub. When Alexis reclaimed her, she'd been wet and eager to play hard.

But Jane had been beautiful then, her body lean and shapely and unscarred. A credit to her own commitment to fitness and healthy living—which had proved no match for genetics. A credit to Alexis, because at a public party, a sub's good looks reflected on the dominant who was with her or him.

And now Jane wasn't perfect. Not even average, but damaged.

They'd kept playing at home, as much as her body would bear, throughout the long ordeal of treatment and recovery. As long as it was just the two of them, Jane could enjoy entwined pain and pleasure, freedom and restraint. She could trust the desire in Alexis's eyes because Alexis loved her, as she loved Alexis, in a way that delved below the pretty surface. They'd known that long before cancer made everything in their lives uglier.

But other people were a different story. She'd seen the looks on the street as her hair fell out and her face became gaunt—pity, fear, even disgust, as if her illness should be hidden away so it didn't offend others.

Now she'd be exposing a far more graphic reminder of mortality than a bald head.

Alexis understood Jane's fears without Jane saying anything. "You're gorgeous," Alexis whispered, clasping the cuff around her wrist. "You're strong." Alexis ran her hand along Jane's outstretched arm, tracing the muscles Jane had worked so hard to keep in shape before her surgery, muscles that were no longer as defined as they once were. Jane winced, but the sincerity in her domme's voice cut through her panic. Alexis believed what she was saying. Jane might not, but she trusted Alexis, so she breathed the deep, cleansing breaths she'd mastered during treatment, and tried to accept.

"I want everyone to see you," Alexis said, securing the other arm. "You're so beautiful. So tough." She repeated the litany as she wove rope around Jane's torso and hips, supporting and ornamenting her. At first, Jane remained tense, her naked body cold and rigid as Alexis went through formerly familiar rituals. But as the rope and her beloved's hands moved over her skin, she began to warm. To open up. To her astonishment, arousal flickered deep in her belly, not the pulsing desire she once felt when she was on display, but a softer erotic feeling that was as much from pushing past her fears to please Alexis as it was from bondage, exhibitionism, anticipation of public play, or any of her old triggers.

Alexis bent and kissed the curve of Jane's belly, softer now than it once was. Flabby, even, after so long not being able to work out, though she was thinner than ever. She nudged Jane's legs apart and secured her ankles with another set of cuffs, the wide leather acting as a firm embrace. In the past, Alexis could suspend her completely, letting the bonds and the web itself support her weight. But this time, she was letting Jane have the security of the floor beneath her feet.

It cut that she wasn't fit enough, at the moment, to be fully suspended, that it would put too much strain on her upper body. At the same time, she was grateful for Alexis for not waiting for her to be that fit again, because it might never happen. They'd had to remove muscle to save her life. Feet on the floor, ropes around her, Jane felt how Alexis accepted her changed body, and that helped her to do so.

Alexis rocked back on her heels. "Radiant," she breathed. Jane didn't understand what she meant. But when Alexis pressed her face against Jane's pubic mound, Jane surged with desire and no longer cared if she understood.

Then Alexis began to lick and finger her, driving her hard and fast toward orgasm.

In the past, Alexis would leave Jane needy and craving when she was a party decoration, letting the gaze of others push her ever higher without driving her over the edge. She'd let Jane come only with her, and only after the display was over and they were flogging and spanking and fucking.

Never like this.

Never before the party even started. Never on her tongue, a tender intimacy reserved for the privacy of their bedroom. It marked this time as different, a new beginning.

When Jane begged, "Please, may I come?" Alexis intoned, "Yes," and Jane shattered.

No, she had been shattered and she came together on Alexis's tongue, all the shards resolving into someone brighter and braver than she had felt since she'd heard the words *breast cancer* and then *invasive* and *mastectomy*.

Alexis kissed her way up Jane's body, lingering at the scars where her left breast used to be. A protest fluttered on Jane's lips—she'd never let Alexis kiss her there before, not even at home. Here there were other people around, putting the last touches on setup before the doors opened. Jane knew them all. They were friends, had visited her in the hospital and helped keep Alexis sane during the worst times, but she still felt self-conscious about attention being drawn to her scars.

But heat spread from Alexis's lips and tongue right into Jane's heart, and some long-held tension snapped inside her. Tears streamed down Jane's face, but they were good tears, cathartic tears, and she didn't try to hold them back.

"My lovely survivor. So proud of you," Alexis whispered. "Want everyone to see you didn't let cancer win."

"Welcome back, Jane," someone called from across the room.

And "looking great!" someone added.

But as Alexis wrapped the final hemp rope around her, first above and then below her beautiful scars, the mark of a survivor, Jane had eyes and ears only for her lover.

BAD GIRLS AND SWEET KISSES

Radclyffe

"I thought you were going out on the lake with Mike," Tess said to Leslie as she watched her pull on a pair of hip-hugger jeans and thick-soled black boots. "I think you're going to be too warm out on the water in that."

"I told Mike I'd catch up with him later," Leslie said, leaning toward the mirror hung on the wall over the small vanity opposite her bed. The warm June afternoon breeze came through the open window, carrying the scent of pine needles and lake water, ruffling her shoulder-length, sun-kissed blond hair. She caught it back in a careless ponytail that made her sculpted cheekbones look even more model worthy and met Tess's gaze in the mirror. Her aqua blue eyes sparkled. "Dev promised me a ride around the lake on her motorcycle this afternoon."

"She's the one who brought you home last week when you were late working on the school paper, isn't she?" Tess remembered the dark-haired girl in the leather jacket on the big motorcycle. She'd only seen her for a few minutes, and when Leslie had asked the girl to stay and meet Tess, she'd shaken her head, muttered something that Tess hadn't been able to hear and roared away.

"Yes, she's the one."

"Did she work on the paper too?"

"Dev? No, if Dev had her way, she wouldn't even show up at school." Leslie laughed and rummaged around on the vanity. After opening a tube of lipstick, she swiped her full lips with the light pink gloss and smiled as if enjoying a private joke. "Dev is kind of a bad girl. Hopefully she'll stick around long enough to graduate."

"I can't believe it's over sometimes." Tess doubted her experience in the small rural high school compared to Leslie's, but the ending represented the same thing—the first step toward the future and a life of her own.

"I am just *so* glad that's all over." Leslie swung around and grabbed the big leather bag she carried everywhere. "I don't know why we have to go a week longer than all the other schools around here. You're so lucky you got out early."

"I'm just glad I had this job waiting and could move up here right away," Tess said, the feeling of freedom something she hadn't known she'd wanted until she'd arrived at Lake George to work for the summer at Lakeview, the resort Leslie's family owned. She loved the farm and got along all right with her distant, somewhat sullen stepfather, and she'd never really thought about being anywhere else. But now that she was here, living in her own apartment—even if she was sharing it with another girl working there for the summer too—she'd come to savor the sense of being on her own, making her own decisions and experiencing the excitement of meeting new people in a matter of days. Leslie Harris was practically an instant friend— they'd connected the moment they'd met, even though Leslie was the daughter of the resort owner and not a chambermaid like Tess. Leslie was warm and funny and open and welcoming, and Tess already looked forward to all the time they would spend together before Leslie went off to college and she went home to go to the community college and work the farm.

"Well," Tess said, squeezing out of the way as Leslie hurried past her toward the stairs, "the motorcycle ride with Dev sounds like a blast."

Leslie sent her a blazing smile over her shoulder. She didn't act this excited when she was going out on a date with Mike. "It's going to be great. I've really been looking forward to it."

Tess heard the sound of the motorcycle roaring down the drive and followed Leslie out onto the wide wooden porch and down the steps to the stone path. As Leslie hurried across the grass, Dev slowed the bike, putting a leg down on either side to steady it while Leslie climbed on behind her. Dev handed her a helmet she'd detached from a clip on the back, and Leslie slipped it on, wrapped her arms around Dev's waist and leaned her cheek against Dev's shoulder. Tess got a funny feeling in her stomach watching them, and for a second, loneliness crept in. She'd recognized the low ache in her midsection, having felt it most of her life. She had no siblings, had always been too busy for friends and had quickly learned her hopes and dreams were something only she could understand.

"Bye, Tess!" Leslie waved, her expression joyous.

"See you!" Tess waved back and shook away the melancholy, enjoying Leslie's pleasure secondhand.

Climbing back to the porch, Tess leaned on the railing and looked down the sloping green lawn to the lake where speedboats made graceful curves on the surface as they navigated around the islands that dotted the broad expanse of water. She hadn't had a chance to spend much time on the water, but she loved the way it looked and sounded and smelled. She loved everything about the lake, its constantly changing colors, the dense evergreens that grew right down to the waterline, the still-wild nature of the undeveloped forest preserves all around it.

Other than the few guests, early arrivals to the season, she had the lodge to herself. As soon as she and the other girls had finished cleaning the cabins and lodge rooms for the day, the girls had left to meet their boyfriends in town. With Leslie gone and her work finished, Tess didn't have anything to look forward to for the rest of the afternoon and evening except her own company, which she was used to, after all.

She'd picked up a book in town the other day and was looking forward to reading it. The cover had caught her eye—two young women leaning close, as if they were sharing a secret, or about to kiss. The blurb on the back intrigued her—something about the way it was phrased made her think the women had a romantic relationship. The idea was exciting, and had been for a while. She just hadn't been ready to think about it too hard. Now it seemed she thought about other girls all the time.

Ready to see if she was right about the book, she headed down the steps to the basement door of her apartment. She stopped at the door when the sound of the motorcycle returning caught her attention, wondering what Leslie had forgotten. A low-slung motorcycle slashed into sight, its rider bringing it to a sharp halt at the end of the footpath, kicking up gravel and bits of grass. The rider was about Dev's size, but not as lean, and dressed in the same black jeans and boots. Dev had worn a black leather jacket, but this person wore only a black T-shirt.

This person, Tess realized as she slowly walked down the path, was a girl.

When the girl pulled off the motorcycle helmet and shook back thick dark brown hair that fell to her collar, Tess stumbled a step in surprise. The girl, who couldn't be much older than her, smiled at her as if they were good friends and not strangers, and she was—well, she was gorgeous...the unruly hair made her look a little wild, and her chestnut eyes glinted with bits of gold in the sun, like a big cat's, and her face was all angles and soaring lines and...oh god, Tess realized, she was staring!

Blushing, Tess halted a few feet away. "I'm sorry, are you looking for Leslie?"

"No—Dev."

"Oh, she just left. They were going for a ride somewhere around the lake."

The rider rested her hand on her thigh, her fingers fanning along the inside of her leg. She leaned forward casually with her opposite elbow on the handlebar of her motorcycle, regarding Tess as if she was an object of infinite fascination.

"Who are you?" the girl asked softly, making the question sound like an invitation.

"I'm Tess. I work here."

"Doing what?"

"I clean." Tess felt her chin lift of its own volition. That ought to finish whatever curiosity this girl had. You didn't ride a motorcycle unless you had the money to buy it and keep it running, something she would never have—at least not for a very long time.

"Are you done for the day?"

Tess frowned. "What? Why?"

"Well, I wouldn't want to take you away from your job."

"I don't know what you're talking about."

The girl twisted around on the bike and unclipped a black helmet with a narrow leather strap and held it out to Tess. "You need to put this on if we're going for a ride."

Tess stared at the helmet as if it might bite and automatically put her hands behind her back. The other girl laughed and Tess pressed her lips together. "I'm not going riding."

"Come on, it's safe enough."

"The helmet probably is, but I'm not sure you are," Tess said smartly. What was it Leslie had said about Dev—that she was a bad girl? Now she understood—this cocky, way-too-sure-of-herself girl was one too. A bad girl who was already more interesting than anyone Tess had ever met.

The girl grinned, shafts of sunlight dancing in her eyes. "Oh, I'm definitely not safe. I'm Clay, by the way." She held out her hand. "It's nice to meet you, Tess."

Exasperated, annoyed that she would look foolish if she didn't shake her hand, Tess returned the handshake. Clay's hand was bigger than hers, her fingers thicker, warm and smooth and strong. Before Tess could resist, Clay tugged her a little closer to the bike. "Don't forget to put your helmet on, Tess."

"I'm not going anywhere with you."

A dark brow winged upward. "Why not?"

"I don't know you."

"Well, this would be a good way to start."

Tess couldn't turn away, caught in the dazzling light from Clay's eyes, and Clay's gaze skimmed over her face and down her body in a way that no one's ever had before. She felt exposed, and oddly, inexplicably, excited.

"Come on, Tess. I promise I'll return you safe and sound."

All her life, she'd been reasonable and cautious and careful. She'd grown up on a farm where the weather was fickle, and only meticulous planning and the vagaries of luck allowed for success. She'd been taught to be frugal with money, painstaking with her judgment and close with her private thoughts. She wasn't adventurous, she didn't take risks, she didn't long for excitement. Until she looked into those dark eyes and saw a world she'd never dared to imagine.

Jamming the helmet onto her head, Tess took two steps toward the big motorcycle. "All right. What—"

Clay held out her hand. "Climb on behind me, put your feet on the foot pegs, and wrap your arms around my waist. Lean when I lean, and get ready for the best thing you've ever felt."

Tess didn't think. She just held on and let go.

Clay wasn't exaggerating. Every sensation was amplified— the smell of the woods, the brisk purity of the wind in her face, the startling blue of the sky, the heat of the sun on her bare arms. As Clay spun them around the lake on the twisting narrow road, the bike slanting into the curves, the sun glinting through the trees, Tess was one with the world the way she was alone on the farm at dawn, when all the world was fresh and new.

"Like it?" Clay called, glancing briefly over her shoulder. Her grin made Tess's heart lurch in the best way ever.

Tess tightened her hold around Clay's firm waist. "Yes. It's wonderful. You were right."

Clay covered Tess's hand with hers, squeezing lightly. The contact sent a thrill through Tess's chest and into her stomach. Her cheek was against Clay's shoulder, close to the back of her neck, and she could smell her—tangy, sweet, fresh and oh-so-exciting. Clay was the most breathtaking girl she'd ever known.

"If we get caught taking this boat out, I'm going to get fired." Tess looked back up the hill to the lodge. The big porch was crowded with guests enjoying the sunset, but no one seemed to be paying them any attention.

"Don't worry," Clay said, "I'll have you back before anybody even knows we're gone. I brought sandwiches. We'll have dinner on the island. There's supposed to be a meteor shower tonight. And a full moon. It'll be great."

"Well, Mr. Harris did say we were free to use the boats if none of the guests were using them. So I guess technically it's all right."

"See? Nothing to get bent out of shape about." Clay held out her hand. "Come on. Climb in."

Tess settled in the bow of the outboard while Clay maneuvered them away from the dock. Clay rowed them out twenty or thirty feet from shore and started the motor. The outboard was not that large, and with plenty of boats still on the water, no one was likely to notice the sound of their engine. Tess turned her face to the wind and stopped worrying.

Soon they were bouncing over the waves as the sun sank lower, headed for one of the many uninhabited islands that dotted the lake. A few minutes later, they pulled up along a narrow strip of sand, and Clay tied the boat to a tree. She helped Tess climb out of the boat, and they found a clear spot under the pines to spread out their blanket.

"Hungry?" Clay asked.

Tess stretched out on her back, watching the sky turn pink, then red, then deep purple. "Not just yet. It's so beautiful I just want to look."

Clay lay beside her and propped her head on her hand. "Yes. Gorgeous."

Tess smiled, the skin at her throat warming under Clay's gaze. Clay had been looking at her that way a lot lately—like she was special. And sexy. Clay didn't have to say anything to make her feel that way—she just had to look at her with eyes that grew dark and deep. Tess touched Clay's face. "You're not looking at the sunset."

"I know." Clay's grin faltered as she drew a strand of Tess's hair through her fingers. "I've seen lots of beautiful sunsets, but I've never seen a girl as beautiful as you."

"You know," Tess said softly, brushing her fingers over Clay's shoulder, "it seems like I've known you for a lot longer than just a couple of months."

"It feels like you're the only one who knows me," Clay whispered, and she kissed her.

Tess had been waiting for this moment, wondering what she would do, how she would feel, for forever, it seemed. To be alone with Clay, wanting to touch her, having Clay touch her. No one ever had. She wasn't scared, wasn't nervous—well, not too much. Everything about being with Clay felt right. Clay was right—they knew each other.

Tess tugged at the back of Clay's T-shirt and pulled it out of her jeans. Clay's skin was hot, soft and smooth. She ran her hands up and down the strong muscles in Clay's back, and Clay groaned softly. The sound surprised her—Clay was always so strong and self-assured, but the sound, almost helpless, struck at Tess's heart and made her want to hold Clay, to protect her. She stroked Clay's back, and Clay moved on top of her. Their legs entwined. Tess turned liquid inside.

"Tess," Clay whispered, her breath hot against Tess's ear, "I want to touch you everywhere. It's all I've been thinking about forever."

"I want you to touch me," Tess whispered back, and then Clay was unbuttoning her shirt, kissing her neck and her throat and the valley between her breasts. Tess pushed at the waistband of Clay's jeans, wanting Clay's naked belly pressed against hers.

"You feel so good."

"I've never—" Tess gasped.

"I know. I know. It's okay." Clay braced herself on her arms and smiled down at Tess. "You're perfect. You're beautiful. I—I'm crazy about you."

And then she kissed Tess again, so gently, so tenderly, Tess's heart shattered.

Half-undressed, completely naked—body and soul—Tess held Clay close. As the summer sun blazed out in the blue-black waters of the lake, Tess knew what she wanted. Had always wanted.

She wanted this bad girl with the sweet, sweet kisses, and now the bad girl was hers.

ABOUT THE AUTHORS

ELIZABETH BLACK's erotic fiction has been published by Xcite Books (U.K.), House of Erotica (U.K.), Circlet Press, Ravenous Romance, Scarlet Magazine (U.K.) and other publishers. She lives on the Massachusetts coast with her husband, son and four cats.

GUN BROOKE (gbrooke-fiction.com) lives in Sweden with her family in an old cottage located in a Viking-era village. She is a Golden Crown award and Alice B medal winner as well as a Lambda Literary romance finalist. Having written twelve novels to date, she alternates between writing contemporary romance and science fiction.

MERINA CANYON began writing stories when she was six years old and much later earned an MFA in fiction. She delights in roaming through red rock deserts and sleeping under the dark night sky. She is at work on a series of Flash Truth, a romance novel and a book of spiritual amazements. Her stories have appeared in *Best Lesbian Love Stories, Best Lesbian Romance, Sinister Wisdom, Cactus Heart, Pilgrimage Press* and *Fraglit.com*.

TAMSIN FLOWERS writes lighthearted erotica, often with a twist in the tail and a sense of fun. Her stories have appeared in numerous anthologies and usually she's working on at least ten stories at once.

SACCHI GREEN (sacchi-green.blogspot.com) has published stories in a hip-high stack of books with erotically inspirational covers, and she's also edited ten erotica anthologies, including *Girl Crazy*; *Lesbian Cowboys* and *Wild Girls, Wild Nights* (both Lambda Literary Award winners); *Lesbian Cops* and *Girl Fever*.

DENA HANKINS (denahankins.net) writes aboard her boat, wherever she has sailed it. After eight years as a sex educator, she started telling tales with far-flung settings—India, North Carolina, deep space—and continued with a queer/trans romance novel, *Blue Water Dreams,* about magnetism and self-sufficiency.

AXA LEE is an erotica-writing Michigan farm girl who grazes cattle in her yard and herds incorrigible poultry with a cowardly dog. She's written since her grandmother had to spell the words for her. Other work appears in two Go Deeper Press anthologies, *Shameless Behavior* and *Dirty Little Numbers*.

D. JACKSON LEIGH grew up barefoot and happy, swimming in farm ponds and riding rude ponies in rural Georgia. Her passion for writing led her to a career in journalism and North Carolina, where she edits breaking news at night and writes lesbian romance stories by day.

LT MASTERS lives in the Midwest, where she indulges in the mysteries of life, nature and her passion for photography.

KARA A. MCLEOD is a badass by day and a smartass by night. Or maybe it's the other way around. A Jersey girl at heart, "Mac" is an intrepid wanderer who goes wherever the wind takes her.

JL MERROW (jlmerrow.com) is that rare beast, an English person who refuses to drink tea. She writes across genres, with a preference for contemporary gay romance, and is frequently accused of humor. Her novella *Muscling Through* was shortlisted for a 2013 EPIC ebook Award.

DESTINY MOON is the author of two novels, *Amply Rewarded* and *All I Ever Wanted*, published by Totally Bound. Her stories can also be found in *The Mammoth Book of Quick and Dirty Erotica* and *The Mammoth Book of Best New Erotica 13*.

GISELLE RENARDE (donutsdesires.blogspot.com) is a queer Canadian, award-winning erotica writer, contributor to more than 100 short story anthologies and author of juicy books like *Anonymous, Nanny State, Kinksters* and *My Mistress' Thighs*. Giselle loves a geeky girl and lives with two bilingual cats.

TERESA NOELLE ROBERTS writes for romantic perverts of all sexual preferences. Her short fiction has appeared in *Best Bondage Erotica 2011, 2012, 2013* and *2014; Best Lesbian Erotica 2014; Twisted: Bondage with an Edge; The Big Book of Bondage* and other blush-inducing titles.

L.C. SPOERING (lcspoering.com) lives and writes in Denver, Colorado. Her work has appeared in anthologies with Cleis Press, Lady Lit and Seal Press, as well as *The Dying Goose* literary magazine, and her first book, *After Life Lessons*, co-authored with Laila Blake, was released in 2014.

NELL STARK is the author of the Lambda Literary romance finalist *The Princess Affair* and other works. She chairs the English, Philosophy and Religious Studies department at SUNY Rockland Community College. She and her wife live, write and parent their child just a stone's throw away from the Stonewall Inn in New York City.

REBEKAH WEATHERSPOON was raised in southern New Hampshire and now lives in Southern California with an individual who is much more tech savvy than she ever will be. Her novels include the Lambda Literary finalist *At Her Feet* as well as *Better Off Red* and *Blacker than Blue*, all published by Bold Strokes Books.

ABOUT THE EDITOR

RADCLYFFE has written over forty-five romance and romantic intrigue novels, dozens of short stories and, writing as L.L. Raand, has authored a paranormal romance series, The Midnight Hunters. She has also edited *Best Lesbian Romance 2009* through *2015* as well as multiple other anthologies.

She is an eight-time Lambda Literary Award finalist in romance, mystery and erotica—winning in both romance and erotica. A member of the Saints and Sinners Literary Hall of Fame, she is also an RWA Prism, Lories, Beanpot, Aspen Gold and Laurel Wreath winner in multiple mainstream romance categories. In 2014, she received the Dr. James Duggins Outstanding Mid-Career Novelist award from the Lambda Literary Foundation. In 2004 she founded Bold Strokes Books, an independent LGBTQ publishing company, and in 2013, she founded the Flax Mill Creek Writers Retreat offering writing workshops to authors in all stages of their careers.

More of the Best Lesbian Romance

Buy 4 books,
Get 1 *FREE**

Best Lesbian Romance 2014
Edited by Radclyffe

Filled with stories of intimacy and desire, *Best Lesbian Romance 2014* reminds us of the most wonderful thing about love: endless delight. The happily-ever-afters within these pages embrace a range of scenarios that are sure to arouse and inspire.
ISBN 978-1-62778-010-0 $15.95

Best Lesbian Romance 2013
Edited by Radclyffe

Radclyffe, the *Best Lesbian Romance* series legendary editor and a bestselling romance writer herself, says it best: "Love and romance may defy simple definition, but every story in this collection speaks to the universal thread that binds lovers everywhere—possibility."
ISBN 978-1-57344-901-4 $15.95

Best Lesbian Romance 2012
Edited by Radclyffe

Best Lesbian Romance 2012 celebrates the dizzying sensation of falling in love—and the electrifying thrill of sexual passion. Romance maestra Radclyffe gathers irresistible stories of lesbians in love to awaken your desire and send your imagination soaring.
ISBN 978-1-57344-757-7 $14.95

Best Lesbian Romance 2011
Edited by Radclyffe

"*Best Lesbian Romance* series editor Radclyffe has assembled a respectable crop of 17 authors for this year's offering. The stories are diverse in tone, style and subject, each containing a satisfying, surprising twist."—*Curve*
ISBN 978-1-57344-427-9 $14.95

Best Lesbian Romance 2010
Edited by Radclyffe

Ranging from the short and ever-so-sweet to the recklessly passionate, *Best Lesbian Romance 2010* is essential reading for anyone who favors the highly imaginative, the deeply sensual, and the very loving.
ISBN 978-1-57344-376-0 $14.95

Ordering is easy! Call us toll free or fax us to place your MC/VISA order.
You can also mail the order form below with payment to:
Cleis Press, 2246 Sixth St., Berkeley, CA 94710.

ORDER FORM

QTY	TITLE	PRICE
_____	_____	_____
_____	_____	_____
_____	_____	_____
_____	_____	_____
_____	_____	_____
_____	_____	_____
_____	_____	_____
_____	_____	_____

SUBTOTAL _____

SHIPPING _____

SALES TAX _____

TOTAL _____

Add $3.95 postage/handling for the first book ordered and $1.00 for each additional book. Outside North America, please contact us for shipping rates. California residents add 9% sales tax. Payment in U.S. dollars only.

* Free book of equal or lesser value. Shipping and applicable sales tax extra.

Cleis Press • Phone: (800) 780-2279 • Fax: (510) 845-8001
orders@cleispress.com • www.cleispress.com
You'll find more great books on our website

Follow us on Twitter @cleispress • Friend/fan us on Facebook